Team ADVENTURE CLUB

Captain Cutthroat's Revenge

Team ADVENTURE CLUB

Captain Cutthroat's Revenge

Joe Davison

4 Horsemen
Publications, Inc.

Table of Contents

CHAPTER 1

T he main hallway to Belleview Heights Middle School sits quietly. The large banner that reads "LAST DAY OF SCHOOL" hangs high, motionless between the eggshell-colored brick walls. The red lockers sit closed, padlocks firmly in place. The red ribbon that is tied to the air vent flaps in the steady cool breeze as the air blows. The jingle jangle of keys breaks the silence as Mr. Wellz, the janitor, walks out into the hallway. He looks the halls up and down, pondering where all the children are.

He sees his yellow mop bucket. Limping over to it, he grabs the wooden mop resting in the bucket. He pushes it slowly to the center of the hallway with a loud squeak as the wheels stick and wobble. Mr. Wellz, who looks just about one hundred years old, dips the mop into the already dirty water before he stops to look at his watch. As he does, the big hand clicks on the number twelve while the little hand rests on the three.

The school bell rings so loudly and violently that Mr. Wellz jerks, uncontrollably slinging the mop out of his hand and splashing water out of the bucket. The classroom doors burst open and the happy, over-excited middle schoolers pour out into the hallway like a breached levy during a hurricane. Mr. Wellz raises his arms to protect himself and screams as the sea of preteens overwhelms him and he's sucked into the raging river of backpacks and Trapper Keepers. He is literally carried out of the building to no accord of his own.

As the tide dissipates, Mr. Wellz is left on the ground, missing his left shoe. He quickly checks for injuries, then lies flat on the ground breathing heavily. "Guess, I'll lie here until someone finds me," he says out loud in an old raspy voice. He rests his head on the ground, looking up at the trees. "Well, at least the trees are pretty."

A familiar young female face peers down over him with a wide smile, oversized eyeglasses, and curly dark hair. It's Ms. Doogan, the school's librarian. Her curly hair dangles down like ornaments on a Christmas tree.

"Mr. Wellz, you should have brought your surfboard. It takes all year for those kids to move that fast." She giggles and reaches down, helping Mr. Wellz to his feet.

"Well, thank you, Dottie. I might have just gone to sleep if I had lain there long enough," he says in a jolly tone. "The last day is the most dangerous," Mr. Wellz says, limping away.

Ms. Doogan picks up her stack of books, holding them under her chin. She rushes across campus, through the outside seating area for lunch, down the long concrete staircase by the lunchroom, past the gymnasium, in through a large metal door, up a staircase to the round building, around the never-ending corner to a set of double doors that lead into the school library. Standing there waiting for her is none other than the charming and rather handsome Robbie Whitman, one of the three members of Team Adventure Club.

"Robbie? Why are you sitting outside my library?"

"I wanted to check out that old pirate book for the summer," Robbie says, getting up.

"Oh, into pirates, are ya?"

"Oh, yes, ma'am. I just love them. The battles, the high seas, the gold. But mostly the gold."

Ms. Doogan tries to pull out her keys and is having trouble because she is weighed down by all the books. She sways to one side, almost losing all the books, then over-corrects and sways to the other side. She smiles at Robbie, who watches her for a moment.

"Let me help you, Ms. Doogan," Robbie says, taking the stack of books. But the weight is a little more than he figured it would be and he almost buckles at the knees, dropping all twenty-two books.

"Why do you have so many yearbooks, Ms. Doogan?" Robbie asks with a grunt.

"Every year we take the leftover books that didn't sell and put them in the book storage area. There are yearbooks dating back to 1812, when this school was first established," she says, turning the key to the door.

She opens the door, using her back as she takes half the books off of Robbie's stacks. They both enter the library awkwardly, trying not to drop the hefty stack. Ms. Doogan puts her stack down on a nearby counter, then goes over to the light switch, turning on the lights to the large library.

Robbie puts his stack down on a nearby circular table that is used for group reading. He walks over to the non-fiction section, looking for the book in question. He scans the different shelves, but he can't find it.

"Ms. Doogan, do you know where that pirate book titled *Pirates and Their Big Ol' Booty* is?"

Robbie hears a definitive laugh from across the room. "No sweetie. Let me look it up," she shouts back.

Ms. Doogan walks over to the counter with the computer at it. She starts typing on the keyboard, scanning the list of books that come up. She squishes her eyebrows in confusion.

"It says here it was checked out yesterday. By another student."

"Who?" Robbie asks.

"I can't tell you, Mr. Whitman. So, that's probably gone," she says under her breath.

She continues to read the screen until she gives up and clicks the page off. Tapping her finger on the counter, she thinks for a moment. Then she walks over to the disappointed Robbie.

"You know, I think there might be a few books on pirates in the storage area. If you would like to go take a look," Ms. Doogan says cheerfully.

"That would be awesome!" Robbie smiles widely.

The door to the storage room is actually at the top of a staircase that goes down into a basement.

"You didn't say the storage room was in the basement," Robbie says, peering into the darkness.

"Basement, storage room, same thing," Ms. Doogan says with a smirk.

"Disagree, and I'm sure if I looked up basement and storage room, those would be two different things," Robbie says with wild hand gestures.

"Be that as it may, it's still a storage room," Ms. Doogan says. "But good jobs on nouns." She chuckles.

"Do you have a flashlight?"

"There is a pull string at the bottom of the stairs. Then a little farther in a black switch on the middle column," she says, giving him a little nudge. "There's nothing down there. Let's go." She guides him down the narrow staircase to the bottom. The large room has four large five-tier wooden shelves through the middle, each full of old dust-covered books. On the back wall is more wooden shelving that goes up eight shelves high. There are thick cobwebs that covered the top left and right corners of the shelving. Then, on both sides of the room, there are large laundry bins full of books shoved into corners. In the center of the room is a table for reading, with one large desk light from the 1950s.

"Please show me the pirate books so we can leave," Robbie says, pretending not to be too scared.

"I thought you were in some club for bravery, Mr. Whitman?" Ms. Doogan asks.

"Team Adventure Club is not a bravery club. We are defenders of the earth. And humans. And good aliens..." He trails off. Ms. Doogan chews on her cheek, eyeing him.

"Here is a stack of books, Robbie. These might be them." Ms. Doogan shows Robbie a stack of books lying flat on an old desk.

Robbie picks up the top book; it reads *Tales of Blackbeard*. He thumbs through it, but he puts it back on the table in the center of the room. He picks up another. It reads *Captain Hugo and the Monsters of Terror Island*. Robbie puts it on the table. He picks up another book; this one has a painted picture of a giant red Octopus wrapping its tentacles around a huge white pirate ship. He puts it down on the table.

"You don't like any of those?" Ms. Doogan asks.

"No, those are like kids' books. And I own *Tales of Blackbeard*." Robbie sighs.

"Oh, I know. Come over here," Ms. Doogan says, walking to the far back of the room.

"You know, this is my first year here. So I still don't know where everything thing is," she says, making her way through the cluttered room.

"I know. I'm sorry about your mother. She was the best librarian we ever had." Robbie grins.

Robbie catches up to her as she pulls out a huge wooden traveler's trunk. There is a large latch on the front, but no lock. Ms. Doogan opens the trunk and dust flies into the air. They both cough and Robbie waves the particles away from his face.

"She was just great! I had to pick up where she left off," Ms. Doogan says, pulling a small book out of the trunk and holding it up into the light. "No."

"So you just took over?" Robbie asks, scanning the room.

She pulls out another book, holding that into the light. It's a little bigger in size, about six inches by nine inches. It has a star on the cover and reads *A Trial of Errors*. "No," Ms. Doogan says, putting that book down. "Not that easy. I had to apply, and then fight for the position. But my mom worked here for thirty-five years. I couldn't let her just be forgotten."

As she is digging through the trunk, Robbie looks up at one of the top shelves and sees the gold on the corner of a thick book, that is sloppily wrapped in a brown fabric, shine. He walks over to the shelf, trying to figure out a way to get the book down. Then he sees a broom. He takes the handle and ever so gently rocks the book to the edge until it falls into his hands.

"Gotcha!" Robbie says.

Robbie holds the heavy book in his hands as he unwraps the cloth from around the book. The book is in beautiful shape. The corners of the leather-bound book have a gold filigree. The book is twelve inches wide by sixteen inches long and three inches thick. The paper is made of a thin material that seems too soft for paper. On the front cover, there is a circle with the words:

Woolworth Rutledge, aka Captain Cutthroat.

Robbie smiles widely. He almost starts to vibrate, he's so excited about this book. "Can I check this one out?" Robbie squeals.

"Sure. I don't even know how long it's been here," Ms. Doogan says.

"Thank you, Ms. Doogan," Robbie says, rushing back up the stairs. "Bye, spooky basement!" he exclaims, darting out of the room.

Ms. Doogan walks up to her computer, grabbing her scan gun. Then she realizes this book is too old to have a barcode. She thinks for a moment.

"Robbie, just bring it with you when you come back to school next year," she says with a smile.

Robbie hugs the book like it's a new pet, and he gingerly walks out of the library. Ms. Doogan watches him leave. Then she walks over to one of the stacks of yearbooks picking it up.

"Oh man, I should have had Robbie help me take these down to the basement." She sighs, blowing her hair out of her face. "Dottie Doogan, you'd lose your head if it wasn't attached," she says with a giggle. Suddenly her watch beeps with a red flashing light. She looks around, checking her surroundings.

Talk about a close call, she thinks to herself, then taps on the screen.

"Hi sweetie," she says, walking away.

CHAPTER 2

arrie Calusa, a cute bright-faced, red-haired girl sits on a concrete wall in Belleview Park, wearing her favorite jeans, her favorite rock band tee-shirt, which was Rage the Dragon, and her favorite sneakers, waiting on her two best friends in the whole world: Leanne McCallister and Robbie Whitman. Together, they are Team Adventure Club, the little-known squad of heroes that has managed to stop the world from being invaded more than once, fought a giant slime monster named Gary, and found countless missing pets in and around the neighborhood.

Not to mention stopping an evil robot army from reprogramming all the television stations to old-people shows like *Leave it to Johnny* and *The Cowboy Hour*. They also stopped an alien missile from freezing the entire town. But no one knows this. No one knows they are the silent heroes. Carrie likes it that way. She feels like they are superheroes in that manner. Regular kids by day, Team Adventure Club by night, protecting the world. And pets.

Belleview Heights Park, otherwise known as BHP, is a large city park sitting on the coastline facing west. From the beach, the Belleview Heights Park Pier stretches out several hundred feet into the water. The pier itself has a five-hundred-foot Ferris wheel sitting on the southwest side.

That's where Carrie, Leanne, and Robbie spend a lot of time working out plans for their adventures. It's also a great place for them to talk to Uncle Max if he's on a space mission or fighting aliens.

There is the Diving Dolphin roller coaster, which goes out over the ocean, letting anyone on the ride look down fifty feet to the water below. There is also Razzle's Arcade, which has Carrie's favorite stand-up arcade game, Quick Draw's Revenge, a Wild West timed shooter game. She is really good at it.

The park has four large fiberglass animal play areas. There are large killer whales and sometimes you can see their dorsal fins from the park as they swim in the ocean. There is a dolphin slide, a huge sea lion you can ride like a see-saw, and a manually operated tilt-a-whirl that is in the shape of an octopus.

There are four large rope bridges, a merry-go-round shaped like a UFO you can sit in, eight slides, four tunnel slides, three zip lines, ten swings, two three-person swings, a standup swing, and finally an octagonal metal and rope climbing sphere that is twenty feet high.

On the northwest side, there is the city's largest dog park. It has an obstacle course, concrete tunnels for the dogs to run through, a large sprinkler area for them to run and play and get wet, and an artificial pond they can swim in. As you leave, there are huge blow dryers for the dogs to dry their coats.

Carrie's attention goes to a screaming voice from across the park as she looks up to see a trail of smoke and a frantic Leanne holding on for dear life as her OHNO Z1 scooter rockets toward the giant statue of Admiral Chester Lester, the founding father of Belleview Heights way back in 1681.

Leanne pushes the digital buttons on the LED screen on the scooter, trying to figure out why it is speeding out of control. She waves through menu after menu on the screen until she finds the settings menu. Pressing the button, she opens the menu window, then taps on a folder that opens with more folders.

She looks up to see she is almost out of space and is on a straight course for the giant statue. Waving the menu tab open, several program files open up, each in their own folder. She scrolls the screen up until she finds a folder labeled: Override Shutdown. Leanne opens the folder, revealing a large red button, and presses it.

The scooter immediately goes from high speed to slow to a complete stop. The very front of the scooter's lights barely touch the edge of the concrete base of the giant statue. Leanne sighs a huge breath of relief.

"What in the...? I mean, for real though?" Leanne grumbles.

She brushes her hair back behind her head, looking up at the massive statue of a man in pirate clothing holding a large flag with a symbol of arrows pointing in all directions, in a complete circle, then a circle of stars around that, also known as the chaos symbol.

"Why on earth is the emergency safety button located thirty folders deep?" Leanne screams. "Call me back," she continues, then presses a red phone button on the Team Adventure Club communicator, known as TAC-COM, on her wrist. The images blip away.

Carrie rushes up as fast as she can. "Oh gosh! Leanne! Are you okay?"

"Yeah, my thruster keeps on sticking. I think there's an issue with the timing circuit."

Leanne slings her backpack around to her front, unzipping the larger middle part. Reaching in, she pulls out a small orange box and a large adjustable wrench. Opening the orange box, it reveals that it houses a set of various sizes of screwdrivers, a small flashlight, a compass, and a small handheld ax with various hexagon cut-outs for bolts.

She kneels down, opening the back of the scooter's fender panel. She removes it to reveal a series of colorful wires and a large black square that is humming loudly. She pulls out the white connecting tab and the scooter powers off. Then she undoes the screws on the side of the engine panels that cover the back wheel with a small screwdriver to see the thruster. She pulls out the two red wires from the top. She positions the screwdriver into the screw that holds the stabilizing bracket. The bracket pops off and she can remove the five-inch thruster that looks very similar to a jet engine, showing it to Carrie.

"This thing almost got me killed," Leanne says, standing up.

"What are you gonna do?" Carrie asks.

"Take it to Uncle Max and see if he can fix it," Leanne says, putting it in her backpack.

Carrie looks around, scanning for Robbie. "Where the heck is Robbie?"

"I was doing donuts waiting for him, but then my thruster malfunctioned, and I was set on a one-way course to death," Leanne says, putting the fender panel back on.

"Done." Leanne claps her hands together, standing up. She steps on her scooter, flipping a red switch on the handle. The scooter hums to life. A white fingerprint icon blips on. She puts her thumb on the screen, and it gets scanned, powering up the computer on the scooter. The LED screen comes to life. She watches the screen go through its setup windows and, finally, it's rebooted.

Robbie skids to a stop behind them. "Hey, guys! What's going on? Chattin' with Chester here?"

"What took you so long?" Carrie asks.

"I stopped by the library to get a book about pirates."

"That sounds cool," Leanne says, tapping her screen.

"What are you doing?" Robbie asks, peering over Leanne's shoulder, watching her restart her computer.

"My thruster malfunctioned. I had to take it out," Leanne says tapping the side of her bag.

"What? These scooters don't malfunction," Robbie snorted.

"That's what I thought until I almost slammed into the Admiral," Leanne scoffed, motioning to the statue.

"What did Uncle Max say?" Robbie asks as he balances on his scooter.

"We haven't called him yet. I think he's in the Antarctic for six months," Carrie says.

"Secret Space Mission?" Robbie asks with a wink.

"Hot air balloon race," Carrie replies.

"That's even cooler!" Robbie shouts. "I love hot air balloons!"

Leanne's scooter is ready. "Let's go, guys!" Leanne says, hopping on her scooter and zipping off down the sidewalk.

Robbie and Carrie take off after her. Robbie pulls up a window on the scooter's computer screen, tapping a red button. The screen reads "Thruster Ignition." He presses it. The back fender of the scooter lifts up as the small five-inch thruster pops out, then fires up. The blast shoots Robbie and his scooter past Leanne as he laughs. "Mine works!" he screams.

Carrie laughs as she catches up to Leanne, keeping pace with her. They cruise down Main Street, toward the east side of town, headed toward the center of town. They pass several storefronts, like "Mary's 2nd Hand Thrift"— Leanne's favorite store. She eyes it as she cruises by.

"Hey, guys..." Leanne starts but is interrupted by both Carrie and Robbie, who scream "NO!"

They know exactly what she wants. "Can we stop ..." she begins again but again she is interrupted by the two friends with a unanimous, "NO!"

Leanne shakes her head. "Do you two just hate me?" she asks in a fake cry.

Robbie looks at his watch and it reads 3:50. "Guys, we have ten minutes to get to Second Scoops for 'the last day of school free ice cream cone day,'" Robbie says.

They cross over Central Ave. and the iconic ice cream shop is visible from atop the hill they are about to descend. Robbie loves looking at the fat little ice cream person made of ice cream sitting in a small sugar cone on top of the blue, pink, and purple pastel-colored building. They speed down the steep hill to their destination. Carrie leans against her handlebars, letting go with both hands as she coasts carefree down the hill. She closes her eyes as the cool breeze, which smells like the ocean, blows through her hair. She can feel the sun beating down on her. She feels warm and happy knowing that summer days are ahead. She can't wait to only do Team Adventure Club all the time.

HOOOOOOONK!

Carrie snaps out of her daydream as she narrowly avoids a full-on impact with a cement truck. She turns her handlebars to the left, going up onto the sidewalk, almost hitting a hot dog cart, her wheels skidding on the concrete. She turns the handlebars again, going back into the street, swerving around a parking meter and an empty bicycle rack. She regains control of her scooter, slowing down as Leanne and Robbie roll up beside her. "You good?" Robbie asks, leaning over to her.

"Yes. I was daydreaming."

They roll up to the front entrance on the sidewalk, hopping off their scooters. They all enter a code into their scooter's LED screen and the lights turn red. Robbie's heart stops as he looks over to the walk-up counter and sees his crush, Deborah Valentine. Robbie's eyes seem to sparkle and little hearts appear around his head like he is in an Anime show. Leanne catches him in his daydream, smacking him on the back of his head. "What ya doing? Stop ogling! She's kind of one of us now."

As the team enters through the gate to the walk-up area, Deborah is exiting through the same gate. "Hey, guys!" Deborah says.

"Hey, girl. What'd you get?" Leanne asks.

"I got a Triple C!" Deborah says.

"A what?" Carrie laughs.

"Triple Chocolate Caramel Crunch with marshmallows, pretzels, and candy corn on a cone," Deborah says.

"That looks so awesome, Debbie. Like, really cool. And I bet it tastes amazing! Like, really amazing. Like you. I mean, you don't taste amazing. I mean, maybe if a zombie tasted you, like, right? I mean, what do you mean, right? Marshmallows, huh?" Robbie says in one breath.

Carrie, Leanne, and Deborah stand in silence watching him short-circuit. "Are you okay?" Carrie asks.

"What? Yeah. Ice cream. I mean," Robbie continued.

"Okay, well, I gotta get home. My dad and I are leaving for the islands in the morning. I really just want to stay home and watch *Paranormal Pets*," Deborah says.

"That's cool, though," Robbie says.

"I guess. We are going snorkeling with dolphins!" Deborah says with raised eyebrows.

"Well, have fun. See you in a few weeks," Carrie says.

Deborah starts to walk away but turns, looking back at them. "Hey, do you guys have any cool adventures happening?"

"Nothing yet. But, usually, the summers are the best," Carrie says.

"Well, call me if you need help," Deborah says.

"I'll call you!" Robbie says.

"Stop," Leanne says to Robbie.

"What? I didn't do anything. I literally want to call her," Robbie whispers.

Deborah leaves, getting into her father's convertible sports car. She waves with a smile and the car speeds off. Robbie turns, looking at the walk-up window as the scoop expert is sliding the window closed. Robbie moves as fast as he can, but it feels like he's stuck in slow motion. But he makes it to the window screaming. "Waaait! No! You can't be closed," he pleads.

The scoop expert opens the window. "I'm not closing. It gets hot in here. We have to keep the window closed at all times," he says with a wide, toothy grin. His nose sticks out a little far and his large glasses sit too far down on his nose.

"Whew! I didn't want to miss the 'last day of school free ice cream cone day' day! I thought it ended at four p.m.," Robbie sighs.

"No, it goes until we close, ten p.m.," the scoop expert says.

"Guys! We didn't miss it!" Robbie shouts to Carrie and Leanne.

"Well, welcome to Second Scoop. I'm Larry. I'll be your scoop expert."

"Larry, I would like the Extreme Peanut Butter and Toffee Crunch Avalanche with marshmallows, chocolate syrup, whipped cream, and sprinkles please!" Robbie says with joy in his heart.

"One E.P.B.T.C. coming right up!" Larry says, turning and closing the window.

Carrie and Leanne walk to the window, sitting down on a bench that looks like a candy sprinkle. Robbie looks down at them with a huge smile. "This is going to be the best summer ever!"

CHAPTER 3

Robbie stands in his bedroom looking out the window as the rain pours down for the third straight day in a row. "This is so lame." He sighs. "I hate hurricanes." The lights flicker in his room.

"We better not lose—" The power goes out. Robbie sighs even louder.

"Don't be afraid, guys. It's just a power outage," Robbie's mother shouts from downstairs.

Robbie taps his watch, and a green dial appears. Robbie moves the dial to the thick green line, symbolizing more power. The backup lights in the house turn on, giving every room full lighting. He double-taps his TAC-COM, dialing Carrie's number. A holographic image appears, floating above the watch, of a phone ringing. Carrie answers, her face lit with darkness behind her.

"Your power go out, too?" Carrie asks.

"Yeah, I activated the backup lights Uncle Max gave us," Robbie says.

"Me, too. My parents are super confused."

"Mine have just learned to play along. They know we are up to something, but they have stopped asking questions," Robbie says.

"As soon as this is over, you guys should come here. Let's discuss this summer's plans. We have to get with Uncle Max and see if we're needed," Carrie says.

"Our TAC-COMs will activate if he needs us," Leanne says, walking into Robbie's room.

Robbie positions his TAC-COM, so Leanne is now in the video call frame.

"I just checked the weather. This is supposed to last until 5 a.m., they said," Leanne says, slurping on a milkshake.

"Hey, where's my milkshake?" Robbie demands.

"I made this early and left it in the freezer, but I don't want it to go bad. Got eat the rocky road, loser!" Leanne laughs in his face.

"Cruel," Robbie says.

Slurping is heard from Carrie's end. Robbie looks at the video to see Carrie also sipping on a milkshake. "How did you get a milkshake? Wait, did you two plan this?" Robbie says, frustrated.

"No, dingus, you called me," Carrie says.

"I don't trust you two," Robbie sneers.

"Nor should you. Bye!" Carrie says, hanging up.

"I'll be your best friend if you make me a milkshake," Robbie pleads.

"I can't. The power is off. So no blender."

"Oh, well, thankfully, we have a fully powered backup battery that will run a small country."

Leanne stares at him for a moment. Then Robbie holds up a small square black box with an electric green decal that reads "Team Adventure Club" across it.

"Plug it into this. I'd like cookies and cream with peanut butter please."

"Well, all we have is vanilla and bananas," Leanne says.

"Fine."

Leanne scoffs, turning and exiting the room. "You're lucky I love you."

Robbie smiles, turning to his backpack that hangs from the wall on a wooden hook. He unzips the large part, pulling out the book he borrowed from the school library. He stares at the cover, admiring the calligraphy of the font—its swooping W's in the Woolworth and the dipping R in Rutledge. He traced the C's from Captain Cutthroat. Robbie scrapes his fingernail against the font and some of the gold foil flakes off. Clearly, these letters were written in gold long ago. He races to his desk, opening the book very carefully so as not to harm any of the pages. The paper is old, thick, heavy, and stained brown, with areas of smudging and bent cracking edges.

Robbie scans the pages, reading about the pirate known as Woolworth Rutledge. One passage says, "The worst pirate ever known to man!" Another reads, "In his fifteen years of piracy, he killed over three hundred men!" Robbie turns a page and reveals a huge drawing of an island. Next to the island are several numbers that seem to be just random nonsense. As Robbie continues thumbing through the book, he falls deeper into the lore of the dread pirate Captain Cutthroat. He sailed for years fighting the British Navy, the Asian pirates, the African pirates, and every other pirate there was.

"Here!" Leanne says, startling Robbie.

"Man!" Robbie says, jumping. "Why did you do that?"

"Do what? I walked into your room with *YOUR* milkshake that *I* made!" Leanne huffs.

"Sorry, I was reading about this amazing and horrible pirate. It says he stole millions of dollars' worth of gold and jewels and was never seen again. Some people think he's a myth. Some people think his ship is cursed and is still sailing the seas today!" Robbie says, between taking huge sips of his milkshake.

"That's the problem with folklore. You don't know what's real and what's fake. I guess it's all real to a point. But then people like to embellish the truth a little. So, like a knight who found a sword in a swamp becomes the king who was given the sword by a magic water fairy," Leanne says.

"You're talking about King Author. And he was real. But, yeah, the Lady in the Lake thing is a bit sus," Robbie says.

"But I like pirates, too. Like those ones with that guy who plays that other guy with the scissors fingers," Leanne says.

Robbie stares at her for a moment, not fully believing that she doesn't know the name of either of those films. Or that actor's name. "How are you my sister?"

"Our parents got married."

"Oh, yeah."

"Enjoy your pirate book," Leanne says, trailing off as she walks down the hall.

Robbie reads for hours as the storm rages on outside, the wind slamming the sides of the house. Never is his concentration disrupted. He is laser-focused on every word in every story. The world of Captain Cutthroat is one filled with sword fights, sea battles, and a lot of Aztec gold. Robbie turns a page, reading the caption:

Never before was there such a criminal as that of Captain Cutthroat. He is as vile as he is villainous. His complete lack of regard for humanity leaves little to the imagination. He must be stopped at once and I, King George the XXIII of Argentina, demand his head immediately. I beset a bounty of one million pesos to any man, woman, or child who brings me his head.

Signed
King George the XXIII
of Argentina, 1781

Robbie continues reading page after page. Each story grows in extravagance and is more daring than the last. There are even stories of Captain Cutthroat killing a sea monster three times the size of his ship, The Blasted Dragon, which was recorded as being one hundred and sixty-five feet long, and one of the biggest brig class ships known to be used by a pirate.

Robbie reads until his eyes close and he falls asleep with his face in the book sitting at his desk. The lightning flashes outside, the wind howls, and the drool drips from his lips to the pages of the book. It's a wonder he doesn't suffocate inside the pages with his nose pressed into the crease, basically closing off his nostrils.

Robbie slips off into dreamland. The face of Woolworth Rutledge flashes before him.

The waves raise and lower The Blasted Dragon up and down like a sea saw. The leather boots of a drenched sea pirate stomp the deck of the battered vessel.

"Man the main hoist. Drop those sails! That wind will snap the mast. We're in for it, men! Hold tight or go swimming!" the gruff Captain Cutthroat yells against the thunder.

A thin pirate with a long black beard grabs a rope, twisting it around the cleat on the banister as the bow tilts downward, riding the wave. Other pirates hold on for dear life. The wind pushes the rain into the weathered men with sheer aggression. The stinging rain hits them everywhere. But Captain Cutthroat stands on his deck, arms positioned at his side, with his fists on his belt. He makes riding the waves look easy. The rope holding the boom arm snaps, releasing the large wooden beam. It swings across the deck, hitting a pirate and knocking him into the water. Captain Cutthroat dives, rolling out of the way of the two-ton arm of death that swings wildly.

The rope for the boom jerks and snaps in the wind. Captain Cutthroat draws his rapier charging the foremast, where the rope is twisting around, as a barrel rolls toward him. He leaps on the barrel, launching himself at the boom on the foremast, grabbing the rope, and cutting it free, releasing the damaged boom into the deep ocean. However, the rope he is holding yanks him outward toward the sea. He swings around the ship in a wide berth over the huge waves, his crew watching in awe. As he swings to the stern of the ship, he lands perfectly on the quarterdeck next to the wheel, tying the rope around the cleat on a nearby banister.

Then he turns his attention to the wheel as it spins out of control. Thrusting his rapier through the arms of the wheel in an attempt to stop it from spinning out of control, he damages the wheel arms, cutting through some and snapping others, but the wheel stops spinning. He grabs it with both hands, turning and yelling, "Robbie! Grab my sword. Find the gold. The legend is true."

Robbie is now on the quarterdeck with Captain Cutthroat in the middle of a hurricane.

"What?" Robbie asks, his voice shaking.

"The sword! Pull it out! The sword is the answer!" Captain Cutthroat yells over the lightning.

Robbie pulls the sword out, looking at it. There are several numbers engraved on the metal. Robbie stares at the sword as the ship is hit with a massive wave, pushing almost every box and container overboard. Thankfully, none of the men are swept away.

"Robbie, go now!" Captain Cutthroat roars.

Robbie stares at the sword. It shimmers in the lightning as the electricity splits the sky, striking the ocean with an ear-shattering crack.

"Robbie? Robbie? Robbie?" The voice of Captain Cutthroat transforms into the soft voice of Robbie's mother. "Robbie? Wake up, dear. You fell asleep at your desk. The storm is over. We made it," she continues.

Robbie snaps awake, wiping the drool from his mouth. He suddenly realizes his revelation in his dream. Thumbing hurriedly through the book, he looks at the drawing of the mysterious island. Then he looks at the numbers going across the top of the map: 279759. He flips through the pages again, looking for an image of the sword. Finally, he finds it. There they are, numbers engraved on the sword. But they are too blurry to read.

Robbie turns to his phone, looking up the sword on the internet. "Thank god for Fast Track, the fastest browser known to man."

He looks at the images and finds one in high resolution. He expands the image and there they are. Plain as day. Six numbers: 825033, accompanied by the letter W.

"What do these numbers mean?" Robbie asks out loud.

CHAPTER 4

The large office building of Hedgestone Inc., sits directly in the middle of Chicago. The sleek metal stretches upward one hundred and five floors, just three floors shy of the Sears Tower. The design of the building is hexagonal, with glass on all sides and exterior elevators on the seams of each side. It's a large, national landmark for sightseers worldwide. Riding in the elevator is the best part. You watch as you rise one hundred stories into the air. The last five floors are inaccessible to the public.

The office of the owner of the building, one Sir Oliver Hedgestone, is the entire hundred and fifth floor. The floors are made of marble, as are the six fifteen-foot columns that section off the entire room. There is a sitting area with two red leather couches with chrome trim, which match the two loveseats of the same design. There is a workout area with more equipment than a Gold's Gym, complete with a walk-in sauna.

Sir Oliver Hedgestone's office sits behind the large white wall with the extra-wide double wooden doors at the far side of the floor. The elevator door opens and a tall, thin, bald man in a pastel blue suit with an electric grid check tie, matching pocket square, and custom leather dress shoes imported from Italy steps off.

"Sir, I put the reports on your desk. There are three to review and sign. Also, the wooden Nigerian statue was delivered to your home in London," Gretchen Anderson says. She is Hedgestone's newest assistant. Her healthy, dark, shiny, straight, black hair hangs down to her shoulders, and she has short, straight bangs that hang off her forehead. As they walk across the large room, she adjusts her thick, cat eye eyeglasses. From a distance, she resembles Wednesday Addams.

"Also, this is interesting," she says, handing him a printout of a map.

"What am I looking at?" Hedgestone asks.

"We received this in a package. One of your drone satellites found it. It's an island that used to be a volcano. Island of Hyawhi, off of the Paxio coast," Gretchen says.

Hedgestone stares at it for a moment, examining the details of the island. It is several miles wide, with a large mountainous volcano sitting on the far west end. Hedgestone can tell that the volcano is at least two miles high. Rifling through the rest of the folder, he sees images of the volcano from every side except from underwater. Then, as he flips through image after image, he sees that there is something inside the volcano.

"Is that a ship? Who else knows about this?"

"I don't exactly know, sir," Gretchen says.

"What do I pay you for? Find out. Send Daniel Thornberry and his team there to go inside and take pictures and get back to me ASAP! You'll find his number in your red phone in your office," Hedgestone says, handing the folder back to Gretchen.

Hedgestone turns, stepping onto a long black rubber mat that stretches past and under his office door. "Now!" he demands. Then the rubber mat starts to move as Hedgestone stands on it. Gretchen watches as the mat becomes a conveyor belt of sorts, moving Hedgestone toward his closed office doors. Gretchen watches as the belt moves slower than walking. Hedgestone stands upright as the slow-moving belt ushers him to his office. The double doors swing open and Gretchen can see that the belt goes right up to his desk. Hedgestone looks over his shoulder, back at his new assistant. "Only poor people walk. Remember that," he says as the doors close behind him.

The elevator door dings behind her, startling her. She walks over and gets in. "Guess I'll just walk everywhere," she says with a sigh.

The elevator doors close. She scans her ID card and the buttons light up. She presses the number ten, and the elevator dings as a voice declares over the speaker, "Going down." Gretchen stands silently in the small metal box for a few seconds. She doesn't even have time to look at the folder before the elevator dings and the doors open to the tenth floor.

"This elevator is fast!" she says to a businessman standing on the floor waiting.

Stepping out, she makes her way onto the tenth floor where her office is, along with anyone who works in the top secret division of Hedgestone Incorporated. It, too, is large and fancy. The main reception area has several couches. Most of them are red or black. The reception counter has a marble base and a red cedar top. Becky, the receptionist, is in her fifties and has worked here for fifteen years already. She knows everyone. Her smile is wide and her graying blonde hair, which is pulled back into a bun, makes her look distinguished and educated. She smiles at Gretchen as she passes her.

"Good afternoon, Ms. Anderson. I trust he was in a good mood," Becky says.

"I don't think he's ever in a good mood. Just always in constant hostile takeover mode," Gretchen says with a smirk.

"I do not want to be his enemy," Becky smiles confidently.

"Facts," Gretchen says, taking her memos out of Becky's hand. There is a table in the corner with four leather office chairs around it. As she walks down the hall to her office in the back corner, she passes several other offices with busy employees all doing important business stuff: filing papers, making copies of other papers, and putting papers in folders. One businessman is getting fitted for a suit right in his office.

Gretchen walks into her small corner office that looks out over the city, going up to a large window and looking out as a bright red helicopter that reads "Hedgestone Inc." on the side suddenly appears, blasting past her and up to the roof. She presses her face against the glass to watch the helicopter land on the roof. After a few minutes, she pulls her face off the glass and resumes her duties. Spinning her office chair around, she takes her place in it. Resting the folder on her lap, she starts looking through it.

"What is that? A ship? This is the craziest job I've ever had," Gretchen says.

She picks up a red cell phone on her desk, unlocking it with an eye scan. Opening the contacts menu, she scrolls for Daniel Thornberry's information. She finds it.

CHAPTER 5

Mrs. Calusa opens the door to their house to see Robbie standing there with a stack of papers in his arms. "Where is Carrie?"

Robbie bursts into the house like a man on a mission. "In her room, maybe?" Mrs. Calusa says darting out of his way.

Robbie scuttles up the staircase to the second floor, running to Carrie's room. He pounds on the door, but Carrie doesn't answer. Robbie knocks again, and the door opens a little. Now, he can see that Carrie is in the middle of a conversation with Uncle Max, who is on a digital 3-D hologram projection standing in the middle of the room.

"Robbie!" Uncle Max says.

Carrie turns to see him standing there with a stack of papers folded over each other. "What is all that?" Carrie asks.

"Our summer vacation!" Robbie says.

"Our summer vacation?" Carrie laughs.

"It looks awesome! Whatcha got, Robster?" Uncle Max asks.

"Look!" Robbie exclaims as he holds up a map, trying to unfold it. He fumbles for a minute as he keeps unfolding the map more and more. The map is wider than his reach, so he can't hold it out all the way.

"Carrie, hold this," Robbie says, handing her a corner of the map.

Carrie takes her end, holding it up. "What are we looking at, Robbie?"

"It's a map of Bellevue Heights from, like, two hundred years ago."

"Where did you find that?" Uncle Max says, taking a bite of his banana.

"In this amazing book about the dread pirate Captain Cutthroat! It's a map to where his treasure is hidden!"

"Treasure? Like a real pirate treasure?" Carrie asks in disbelief.

"Yes! Like real pirate treasure," Robbie says.

"Mell ush smore, Robshi!" Uncle Max says with a mouth full of banana.

"Okay, so there's this island. Island of Paxio. Off that island, there is a volcano. Somewhere around there is his ship, The Blasted Dragon, and it's full of gold and gems!" Robbie says, running out of breath.

"I love pirates!" Uncle Max exclaims.

"So, you want us to look for treasure?" Carrie asks sardonically.

"Yes."

"I don't know. Mom and Dad want to go on a trip to the Grand Canyon this year," Carrie says with a hint of mocking sadness.

"Okay, guys. I got to go. I'll be in space if you need me. Three weeks on the space station Tides."

"Tides? Isn't that Hedgestone's space program?" Carrie asks with a grunt.

"Kind of. He just put money into it. It's run by a Swedish company, though. He's not really involved," Uncle Max says.

"He hates us!" Robbie says.

"Yeah, well, he knows that there's a group of kids out there who fight for what's right and that no matter how much money he has, he can't stop you guys," Uncle Max says.

"He's ruthless. And evil," Carrie says.

"Facts! I got to go." Uncle Max blips out, and the hologram shuts off just as Leanne walks through Carrie's door.

"Shoot. Was that Uncle Max? I needed to ask him about these thrusters malfunctioning," Leanne says, putting her hands on her hips.

"Yeah, he's going to the Tides Space Station for three weeks," Carrie says, letting go of her side of the map.

Robbie flips the map, laying it across Carrie's bed fully open. Leanne steps in, looking it over. She loves the look of it. It's old, with a sepia hue. Clearly made with a fountain pen. The calligraphy is beautiful as it spreads all over the map denoting names of regions, areas where there are whales, sharks, dolphins, and some sea creature that looks like a snake dragon. She runs her finger across it as both Robbie and Carrie watch her fall into a trance-like state. Her smile says it all. She follows the dotted line leading to an X on the map.

"This is a pirate's treasure map!" Leanne proclaims.

"Yep." Robbie nods.

"Is this our summer vacation?" Leanne continues.

"Yep." Robbie nods again.

Carrie rolls her eyes, giving a sigh. She looks over at the well-used leather satchel hanging on her wall. It's now that she notices a dirty smear of dirt and clay on the bottom of her satchel. She starts to think back to a mission in the jungle where they were in some serious danger. She can hear the sound of the waterfall and suddenly she is there, running from the Leopard Man.

Carrie is in a controlled slide down the muddy mountainside. Looking back, she sees both Leanne and Robbie in slow motion as they both dive over the jungle flora and fauna. Robbie reaches out and grabs a thick vine and swings through the air, whereas Leanne is mid front-flip, Both land next to her and slide down the steep terrain. They reach the edge of the cliff, dropping off and into the back of an older, yellow pickup truck driving wildly. Mud slings everywhere as Uncle Max tries to control the speedy vehicle across the muddy and slick road, spinning the steering wheel one way and then the other, gaining control if ever so loosely.

"We need to get this Tiger's Eye gem back to the Nungon village leader before these poachers kill us all!" Carrie screams from the back of the truck bed.

Robbie turns just in time to see a poacher fall off the cliff onto the muddy road, just missing the bed of the truck. "Ouch," Robbie says out loud. He watches as the man stands up in pain, only to get smeared by a huge mud blob that was rolling down behind them.

Uncle Max shifts gears in the cab of the truck, keeping it on the road if ever so slightly. The edge of the cliff is just under the passenger side wheels. He blows a big bubble as he maintains his confidence.

"Fear not, my little heroes. I have it all under control," Uncle Max says out the driver's side window.

Carrie sticks her leg in through the sliding back window that leads from the bed to the cab. She squeezes her way into the cab sitting next to Uncle Max and quickly puts on her seat belt. Looking up, she sees that the road turns sharply, and she and Uncle Max scream.

"Hold on!" Uncle Max shouts to Leanne and Robbie in the bed.

But it is too late. The truck is going over the edge. The inertia keeps Robbie and Leanne in mid-air as the truck itself drops down about twenty feet. Robbie uses his quick thinking to press the small red button on his TAC-COM to release his grappling hook. The mechanism unlocks with a click and shoots out a long metal cable with a metal claw on the end. The claw slams into the roll bar on the bed of the truck, grabbing it hard and pulling Robbie to it.

Leanne, however, is too far away from the truck now as she flies through the air. Grabbing two para-cords on either side of her backpack straps, she pulls and her backpack opens up like a hang-glider with a THWIP. Using the para-cords, she guides the hang-glider, following the truck down the steep incline.

Robbie lands in the truck with a thud, causing Carrie to look back and see him riding the bed of the truck like a surfboard. She can see Leanne in the air, using her hang-glider several feet above them.

"Slow down a little. We need to let Leanne back in the truck."

Uncle Max looks in the rearview mirror only seeing Robbie, so he sticks his head out the driver's side window, looking around for Leanne when he sees her gliding above them.

"Sweet. That worked?" Uncle Max yells to Leanne.

"Wait. You didn't test this out first?" Leanne screams.

Uncle Max grimaces, pulling his head back inside the truck. "It worked."

"You didn't test the gliders?" Carrie asks holding on for dear life.

The truck bounces over bumps as Uncle Max tries to steer it through the jungle. Branches and vines smack the truck's hood and windshield over and over again.

"Do you know where you're going?" Carrie asks.

"Yeah, this way." Uncle Max points out the windshield.

Leanne is soaring higher now, looking ahead of the truck, watching them. She can see a path three hundred feet ahead of them. She talks to her TAC-COM. "Initiate Bluetooth."

The TAC-COM comes to life, turning on a blue screen. A blue light also appears on the earpiece in her ear. "Call Carrie Calusa," she says, pulling on the right strap, guiding the glider slightly to the right.

Carrie's TAC-COM comes to life as it starts ringing. Carrie and Uncle Max look at the

TAC-COM as Leanne's face pops up. Carrie taps her communicator.

"What are you doing?" Carrie asks.

"Trying not to die. I can see a path ahead of you. Keep going straight," Leanne says.

"Go straight," Carrie says to Uncle Max.

"What?"

"Leanne can see a path ahead," Carrie says.

Leanne keeps an eye on them and the path ahead when she sees another large truck coming at them from the right. "We got company. Go right, now!"

"Go right," Carrie yells to Uncle Max.

As he steers the truck to the right, they pop out of the thick jungle and onto a muddy path. The truck slings up mud and slides to the right, just missing the oncoming truck. Uncle Max and Carrie get a good look at the driver and it's a dirty, long-haired man. His beard is ragged, his face black from dirt, his big, dark eyes peer at them, and he has a rotting, toothy grin. It's Leopard Man, and he is furious.

"He looks happy," Uncle Max says sarcastically.

Uncle Max keeps the truck on the road and steps on the gas. He reaches over to his TAC-COM, pressing a button, and it comes to life.

"Leanne, what do you see?" Uncle Max asks.

"Keep going straight. The village is below us. There's, like, a windy road ahead. You have, like, four turns coming up," she says.

Robbie is in the back of the truck watching Leopard Man make a U-turn, sliding the truck in the mud as the wheels lock up. It gains on them quickly. "We got company," Robbie says, pounding on the back window of the cab. He watches as the madman behind the wheel of the other truck speeds toward them. He rams the back of the truck, causing Robbie to rock and almost lose his grip on the roll bar. He looks in the bed of the truck seeing a few large bags of flour. Grabbing the burlap sack, Robbie picks it up and tosses it at the truck. It doesn't go far, flopping off the truck's bumper and falling to the mud below. The other truck runs over it. Leopard Man looks at Robbie with a confused look. Robbie just shrugs his shoulders and picks up another bag. He waits a moment this time, until the truck is close enough, and tosses it. The heavy bag lands on the hood of Leopard Man's truck. It does nothing to slow the man down.

Leanne looks ahead of them just in time to tell Uncle Max to turn left. "Turn left!"

Uncle Max turns the wheel left, following the narrow path. Robbie almost falls down in the bed of the truck but manages to hold on. Robbie's foot hits something, and he looks down to see a small spare tire. Looks like it's for a small car. He picks it up, and it's lighter than he thought it'd be. He throws it hard at the truck. It hits the hood of the truck, spinning upright and rolling over the windshield, bouncing off the roof. Robbie sighs in disbelief. He looks for something else when he sees a crowbar. He picks that up, flinging it at Leopard Man. It sticks in the windshield, surprising them both. It shatters the windshield, making a cracked spider web across it. But it doesn't bother or impair Leopard Man at all.

"I'm coming for you, Team Adventure Club," he snarls.

Leanne guides her glider over them as she looks for a way off the road but it isn't long before Uncle Max has taken things into his own hands and realizes that if he just goes straight through the less dense jungle, he can bypass the road and make it to the village in half the time. So he turns the wheel and into the brush they go. Leanne watches and knows exactly what he's doing. Leopard Man turns, following him into the jungle again.

"He's still coming!" Robbie shouts.

"We're almost there," Uncle Max says.

Then Leanne notices a huge problem. There is a small river they have to cross, but it looks dangerous and she's not sure the truck will make it.

"There's a river ahead," she yells through her mic.

She looks around and sees the road has a bridge. If Uncle Max continues, he can turn left on the dirt path several yards ahead of them and they will be on the road.

"Uncle Max, when you hit the next dirt path, turn hard left and go to the bridge," Leanne says.

Uncle Max nods, steering the truck through the jungle, crashing through thick trees and palm fronds. What Leanne doesn't see is that the jungle leads them to a ten-foot drop-off before they hit the road. It's too late when Uncle Max and Carrie see it as well.

"Hold on," Uncle Max shouts as the truck roars off the edge.

Robbie is once again floating in mid-air as the truck drops. Using quick thinking, he shoots his grappling hook at Leanne. The hook grabs her backpack tightly, catching him. He is only a few feet ahead of Leopard Man's truck. As it approaches *him, he runs over the hood and roof and then he's in the air again, dangling under Leanne as she soars across the river.*

Uncle Max and Carrie hold tight as the front of the truck slams into the mud, sticking them in like a dart. Carrie and Uncle Max stare at the ground, both screaming like girls. But that doesn't last long as Leopard Man's truck lands on the bed of Uncle Max's truck and somehow pole volts into the river, engine first, making Uncle Max's truck roll onto its roof.

Carrie and Uncle Max crawl out into the mud to see Leopard Man floating in his truck down the river as he screams at them.

"This isn't over, Team Adventure Club!"

Uncle Max and Carrie start running to the bridge and cross it as Leanne and Robbie land on the ground. They are safe.

"Let's return that gem to the village and get out of this country," Carrie says.

CHAPTER 6

Gretchen Anderson sits in the back of the large SUV, reading her tablet. She skims over pictures of the island of Paxio from different time periods, as far back as the 1950s. This strange object looks to have been sitting in the spot, unmoved, leading her to believe that it must be a rock formation that looks just like a ship, and this is a huge waste of time and resources. But what else is a billionaire to do with his money?

"Mrs. Anderson, we're here," the driver says.

Gretchen looks up to see they have arrived at the private airport. The huge hangar in front of her is at least sixty feet tall and three hundred yards wide. She exits the SUV and can see that there are at least six planes and three helicopters inside the hangar. All polished. All in pristine condition. All ready to go at a moment's notice.

An older man with a short, gray beard and a slicked-back haircut walks out to meet her. He is wearing an olive-green jumpsuit that reads "Lewis" on the name tag. His sleeves are rolled up to his elbows and she can see he has military-type tattoos on his forearms. One specifically is of a spaceship abducting a person right from inside a log cabin. It is cool, to say the least. His eyes are accented with crow's feet, and he has a permanent squint.

"Mrs. Anderson. I'm Jacob Mallory. Your pilot," he says, shaking her hand.

"Nice to meet you. I'll assume you've been doing this a long time."

"No, ma'am. First day. I was a professional alligator wrestler for thirty years until yesterday. I hope you brought a life vest," he says with a chuckle. "I've been flying longer than you've been alive, Mrs. Anderson. You have nothing to worry about."

Gretchen smiles and follows the man into the hangar, where they walk up to the largest helicopter she has ever seen. Its black-and-white coloring makes it look just like an orca. Her eyes go wide with intimidation. "This is huge!" she says, as Jacob guides her around the front of the vehicle to the passenger side.

"Yes, ma'am. It's an ACH160. Luxury at its finest. The design team retrofitted the standard doors to our patented sliding doors for easy access. Specialized for our reconnaissance missions. It'll do 148 miles an hour for 500 miles, or better," he says with a wide smile.

Gretchen gets in as she notices a fleet of biplanes sitting in a field. Their yellow and black color makes them look like a group of yellow jackets. She turns to Jacob, smiling as he shuts the wide passenger door.

The back sliding doors to the ACH160 slide open on both sides as four men get in wearing all black, including black ski masks and black military helmets. Gretchen turns, looking at the men in confusion. "Who are you guys?"

None of the men answer her. She smirks and turns back around in her seat. Jacob climbs into the pilot's seat, now wearing a large aviator helmet. "Who are these guys?" Gretchen asks him.

"Recon team," he says, securing his seat belt. "Put on your harness."

Gretchen pulls the straps over her shoulders to a buckle in the middle of the seat, locking the two straps in place. Jacob motions to her to put on her headphones, complete with a microphone. He starts flipping switches and adjusts his joystick as the helicopter comes to life. The four men in the back connect audio cables to the side of their helmets.

"Everyone in?" Jacob asks, looking over his shoulder.

The four men nod. Gretchen smiles and nods. "This is going to be awesome!" she says.

Jacob looks around then pulls back on the joystick and the helicopter lifts up off the ground only a few feet and he guides it out of the hangar. It moves incredibly smoothly and effortlessly as he steers it out of the large building. Once they reach the large airfield in front of them, he pushes a few more buttons and radios the tower.

"Tower V12? This is ACH160—992 set to go," Jacob says.

"992, you are set to go. Clear skies. Enjoy your flight," a filtered voice says.

And like that, the helicopter is air born in seconds. Gretchen's stomach turns a little from the inertia of the liftoff. She holds her stomach for a moment. The feeling subsides. Looking out the window, she realizes they are very high already. And moving quickly.

"Ladies and gentlemen, thank you for flying Air Jacob today. We should reach our destination in about an hour and a half," Jacob says.

The helicopter soars across the skyline of the city toward the ocean. Gretchen looks in amazement. This is the first time she's seen her city from a view like this. And the ocean before them looks amazing as the cresting waves crash against the rocky coast and the white sea foam forms like ice cream mixing with root beer. The horizon takes her breath away. The dark blue water of the ocean meets with the bright blue sky. She is starting to love her job.

Gretchen opens her leather-bound folder, looking at her notes. She scans the history of the volcano. Pulling out the satellite view of the island, she studies it. The image really does look like a pirate ship. But she can't find any evidence that a ship crashed around the island. So it has to be a rock in the shape of a ship. She looks out the window and all she can see is the ocean for miles. It is peaceful and scary.

What if the helicopter crashes? What if there are sharks? How do you fight a shark? What about killer whales? Are they worse than a great white? Gretchen starts to panic and turns her attention to Jacob, who seems to be sleeping. *Is he sleeping?* A million thoughts rush through her brain all at once. She keeps staring at Jacob, trying to see if he is awake or not. It is hard to tell because the sun visor on his helmet is so shiny all she can see is her own reflection. Without realizing it, she has moved within a few inches of his face, staring at her own face.

Jacob flips his visor up, scaring her. Gretchen shrieks, jumping back to her seat and startling herself out of her trance.

"You okay, Mrs. Anderson?"

"What? Oh, yeah. Fine. Why? Should I be worried? You're worried. I'm fine. But what about sharks?" she rattles off like a crazy person.

Jacob stares at her for a moment. "Did you have a panic attack?"

"Maybe. I'm fine now."

"Don't worry about this vehicle, ma'am. It's state-of-the-art. It won't crash even if I die of a heart attack."

"Heart attack?! Are you going to die soon?" Gretchen's palms sweat on her folder.

"No, ma'am. I'm fit as a fiddle."

"How fit is a fiddle? That's the question. Who's measuring these fits on fiddles?" she asks.

"It's fine. Sit back, relax, and enjoy the flight. We got about another twenty minutes and we'll be there," Jacob says.

"Yeah, then we have to go back," she says.

"Just relax. You'll be fine."

Gretchen knows he is right, but she still doesn't trust the helicopter. It is a computer, basically, and computers break all the time. Her laptop can't even open a zip file without three updates and a restart.

"Well, if this thing needs a restart, that'll be bad," she says.

"If thing needs a restart, we'll become a submarine at 100 miles an hour."

The four men in the back of the helicopter laugh out loud and fist-bump each other. Gretchen looks at them. She almost forgot they were even back there. She studies them for a moment. No name tags. They all look the same.

"Why are you guys here again?" she asks.

"Recon, ma'am," the one on the far right says.

"I thought I was doing that?" she says.

"From the 160, ma'am. We are to touch ground and get recon from inside the volcano," the man continues.

"Wait. What? I wasn't told about this," she says.

"I don't know anything about that, ma'am. We were ordered to join the flight," he says.

"Ordered? By whom?" Gretchen asks.

"Mr. Hedgestone. Our boss," he says.

"You work for Oliver Hedgestone?"

"*Sir* Oliver Hedgestone. He's a knight and should be addressed as such."

"Well, yes. But not in mixed company. Seems a bit excessive to also include his title. I mean, we all know he's a knight," she says, trying to cover up her mistake.

"Be that as it may," the man says.

Gretchen just turns around in her seat and stares out the window.

Jacob taps her on her leg, then points out the windshield, showing a small spot on the horizon.

"There it is. We're almost there."

Gretchen leans forward, looking out the windshield, watching the dark spot form into a rocky outline of an island. They approach quickly, and the island grows every second. And then they are upon the island. It is massive. It is three miles high and six miles wide. There is a large jungle at the base of the volcano, but the island is devoid of human life, as the conditions there are not ideal for humans. But the wildlife is bright, beautiful, and exotic. Gretchen watches as a flock of bright red and blue birds flies across the cove at the shoreline.

The helicopter makes a pass around the entire island in what seems like minutes. Gretchen looks out her side window now as the helicopter has tilted to its right, leaning slightly. She can see the ground now and is in awe of the entire island.

"I'm going to approach the top of the volcano and descend into the heart of the beast. We'll find a spot to drop you boys off," Jacob says.

"Roger," one of the men says.

The helicopter rises over the top of the mountain to reveal a large mile-wide crater that drops down at least two miles. It's magnificent. The helicopter drops fast, like an elevator. Jacob spins the helicopter in a circle, looking for a spot to put the men. Finally, he sees an edge with a large area he can get close to. Leveling the helicopter, he lines up along a straight edge of the cliff, motioning to the men.

"That work?"

One of the men slides open the side door with a whoosh. The helicopter rocks a little as the rush of air pushes it sideways.

"Be careful. That is one serious updraft," Jacob says.

One of the men sitting by the door pulls out a metal arm that has a spool on one end. He pulls out a thin black nylon rope from his front pouch, clicking it into place. He nods to his fellow recon specialists, then steps outside the helicopter, dropping out of sight. Gretchen screams a little.

The men on the other side of the helicopter open their door and also clip into a metal arm, dropping out of sight. Gretchen screams again. "Every time. Wow, this is amazing," she says.

The men land on the ground with ease and unlock their cables. Leaving them there.

"Mike and Scott, you two go that way. Junior and I will go this way. Pictures only. He needs proof first. Move out," Jaxx says.

"Yes, sir."

They start down the rocky slopes into the unknown.

Gretchen stays in the helicopter with Jacob, unsure what to do next.

"So, been a pilot long?" she asks.

Jacob smiles wide, then taps a pin on his lapel that reads twenty years of service. Gretchen shakes her head, disappointed in herself that she didn't notice that pin the entire flight there. Jacob's big helmet and black-as-midnight visor hide a lot of his face. He seems old but looks great for his age.

"You sound young for twenty years of service. How old are you?" she asks.

"I've been in one service or the other since I was sixteen. I passed this test once and those involved, let's say, put me in the pilot's seat. I've been there ever since," he says.

"Sixteen, holy moly," she says.

Jacob reaches into a small cooler under his seat pulling out two bottles of water. "Want a water?" he asks.

"Yes, thanks!" she says. "This view is stunning," she says just before she takes a big sip of water.

"How long have you worked for Mr. Sir Oliver Hedgestone?" she asks.

"I don't work for that man. I'm a hired contracted agent. He pays my company for services. If the money wasn't so good, I wouldn't be here. I got a space stat..." Jacob stops himself.

"Were you going to say PlayStation? I have one of those! Love it to death! Do you play *Grapthar's Hammer: Sons of Warvan?* That game is so dope. You're a new space explorer trying to save one planet at a time from bandits and evildoers and..." Gretchen stops talking.

"I haven't played that one. Sounds great! Is that like an RPG sandbox or linear?" Jacob asks.

"Totally open world. Skill trees and everything," she says.

"I play a lot of *Cops and Robbers: Steel City,*" he says.

"That's awesome," she says.

Gretchen's attention changes as she sees a flock of red, blue, and green parakeets soar by.

"Look at that. Wow," she says.

CHAPTER 7

The ship hisses as Uncle Max activates the reverse thrusters. He guides the Falcon One, a large six-passenger spaceship shaped like a football, into the port of the Gillihad Space 8—the largest space station in the Milky Way. The large ship slides into place with ease. Two port hoses extend to the bow of the ship, automatically connecting and securing the ship into place. Then a large, accordion-type antechamber extends to the port door on the side of the ship.

Uncle Max exits his seat walking into the main cabin of the ship where two astronauts greet him. He rubs his messy hair, only to make it messier. Both astronauts are wearing Galactic Federation flight suits. Uncle Max is also in a flight suit, but he wears a blue and yellow hoodie over it. This is the kind of work he's used to, so every day is Casual Friday for him. He motions for the astronauts to follow him.

"Dr. Teller and Dr. Sinclair, this way, if you please," Uncle Max says.

Dr. Teller, an older man with gray hair and a salt-and-pepper beard, nods.

"Do you do this kind of thing all the time?" he asks.

"Yes. Space is my second home," Uncle Max says.

Dr. Sinclair adjusts her suit. Her dark, pixie-cut hair accents her beautiful, dark skin. She leans over, looking out the porthole window at the huge space station. Her eyes say it all.

"Don't worry. This place is amazing. The cafeteria alone is worth the visit. How long are you guys stationed here?"

"I'm here for six months. I had no idea it was this big. How many people are on this thing?"

"Well, I think there's like a hundred *people* on here. But you guys better prepare yourself for other things as well," Uncle Max says.

"Other things?" Dr. Teller asks.

Uncle Max stares at them for a moment. He isn't sure if he is the one who is supposed to tell them about the existence of aliens. It's a tough pill to swallow for most folks.

The door to the cabin pressurizes and opens with a swoosh. A young female in a space station flight suit steps on board. Her insignias mark her as a lieutenant in the Galactic Fleet. She has a nice smile and is younger than all of them. Her flight suit fits snuggly and her side cap has a silver badge that has a center star accented by wings on either side.

"Maximilian. Pleasure to see you as always," Lieutenant Stephanie Rose says.

"Good morning... afternoon, Steph. What's new on this floating space yacht?"

"Same old, same old. Hi, I'm Lieutenant Rose. I'll be escorting you to your duty stations. Or offices, rather, since you're civilians," she says.

"Nice to meet you," Dr. Sinclair says with a smile.

"Pleasure is all mine. We are excited to have two of the world's leading botanists on board the Gillihad," she continues. "Please follow me."

They exit the ship in the antechamber that leads to the interior of the Gillihad. The massive inside is something they are not ready for. It is the size of a mall. Everything is spotless and stainless steel. The floors look like marble and there are huge windows. It is evident they are in space. And they realize they are on the fifteenth floor, which is about the middle of the space station. They are on a catwalk that leads to an elevator, allowing them to see all the way down to the bottom floor and all the way up to the top floor. They are in awe.

"I heard stories of how big this place was, but I had no idea," Dr. Teller says.

"Yes. We have thirty-two floors plus two engine levels and one commander level at the very top. The mess hall is on the ninth floor, and sleeping quarters are on the twentieth floor. I'll show you to your rooms so you can unpack and rest up. You're needed at 0800 hours, so that gives you plenty of time to check the place out. You have yellow security clearance. So levels one through ten and twenty-five through thirty are off limits. Basically, just stick to your level and you'll be fine," Lieutenant Rose says, guiding them across the catwalk.

They stand there waiting for the elevator. It dings and the doors open. Dr. Teller's and Dr. Sinclair's eyes go wide as a small purple creature steps out. Its eyes are almost the size of its head and are bright green. Its mouth is thin until it opens it. Then it is as wide as its head. It is wearing a Gillihad flight suit with three metal insignias on each shoulder. Then there is a small silver button on the collar.

Max high-fives the small alien as Dr. Teller and Dr. Sinclair stand with their mouths open, staring at the alien scientist who, in turn, stares back at them. Lieutenant Rose looks at Max and they both roll their eyes. Often they forget that not everyone has seen an alien, let alone worked with an alien in such close quarters.

"Bremmie, meet your new colleagues: Dr. Teller and Dr. Sinclair," Lieutenant Rose says with a smile and hand gesture.

"You're an alien," Dr. Sinclair says.

"As you are to me. However, we are in space, and therefore we are all aliens to each other. I know as little about humankind as you do about Wookoolians," Bremmie says.

"Woo... Wookoolians? Is that your species?" Dr. Sinclair asks.

"Yes. We come from a galaxy farther than yours, but after the Galactic Battle or the War of Hoovgar, we, as well as Earth, Mars, Espiecsious Galvin 4, and Plutonians, have all banded together for the greater good of the universe."

"Wait. Plutonians? War of Hoovgar?" Dr. Teller asks.

"Okay, guys. There will be plenty of time to catch up on all this. Let's get you guys to your dorms and all set up. Max, are you staying or leaving?" Lieutenant Rose says.

"I'm here for a couple of weeks. I'm working in research and development with Meethorpe."

"Well, shall we?" Lieutenant Rose asks, ushering the botanists into the elevator.

"Steph, wanna get some lunch later?" Max asks.

"Well, I would, but someone invented a new helmet with heads-up tracking lasers and now half of the blue squadron has training all day." She smiles.

"I can't help that I'm a genius," Max says.

Lieutenant Rose smiles at him as the elevator door shuts.

The mess hall, or cafeteria, is large, like a school lunchroom. There is a line of cadets, doctors, and various species of creatures, all waiting for food. Max walks slowly through the cooler area, looking at wrapped sandwiches, salads, snacks, fresh seafood, and items native to all the various aliens onboard the space stations. Max has acquired a liking for *trekfa*, a spicy insect dish from Pluto—beetle-like insects put into a native broth. It is similar to a gumbo you would find on Earth. He points to the *trekfa* and the humanoid alien behind the counter pours it into a bowl.

"You want the *flurga* with it?" the lunch person asks.

"Yes, please."

The chef plops on a heavy helping of the white creamy substance. Max smiles, scooting down the line to the cashier. He flashes his white card and moves on. The cashier presses a button, and the total comes up as zero. Max makes his way across the wide lunchroom as he sees two men walking and talking across the room. Max stares at the men for a moment, then realizes who they are.

Max sits down, watching the men as he digs into his gumbo substance. Max is startled by the smacking of a tray hitting his table. He turns to see Dion, an inventor and developer from research and development.

"Hey, is that John Lewis?" Max asks.

"You mean MMA champion and now astronaut John Lewis? Then, yes," Dion says.

"Why is an MMA fighter on the Gillihad?"

"I'm not real sure, but I think it has something to do with Space 11," Dion says.

"I got to find out." Max stands up, making his way over to the men.

"John Lewis? What a pleasure, sir," Max says.

John, a lean-cut, good-looking, bald-headed man, stands with another lean, good-looking bald-headed man. They are both in civilian clothes and holding cafeteria trays. John nods to Max and smiles.

"You're Maximilian Bonnefield, correct?" he asks.

Max is stunned for a moment as he realizes that John knows his name. He often forgets that he is considered a national hero and everyone who is on the space station knows that without him, and the other survivors of the Galactic Battle, Earth wouldn't be here.

"Yes," Max says.

"Guys, it's Maximilian Bonnefield," John says.

Several more fit men come from around the corner. They look like fighters and soldiers. Max certainly feels overwhelmed. After all, he's not fit, and he doesn't consider himself a hero. He feels more like the fun guy who likes to eat pie.

"Wow. What is happening up here?" Max asks.

"We're building an MMA space area for galactic fighting," John says.

Max's eyes go wide, and he's gob smacked. "Wait. What?"

"My team and I are building an arena over there," John says, pointing out the window.

"It's going to be the biggest event for Earth that has ever happened. Forget the Super Bowl," the other man says.

"Oh, this is my partner, and Space Marine, Cheyenne Buchanan. He's a major in the Galactic Fleet, but also an undefeated MMA fighter," John says.

Max just stares at the man. A real Space Marine in the space station. They never come to the space station. They are never seen by normal people. Their identities are kept secret for the most part because of plausible deniability.

"Max, it is a real pleasure meeting you. You're a real hero," Cheyenne says.

Max mumbles, unable to say real words. He stares at the Marine's tattoos on his neck. Then he looks over the space armor. It's shiny and silver. His chest plate has dents and dings and what looks like claw marks that cut deep into it. Cheyenne notices him looking at the damage.

"Gillihad 1. You're lucky you weren't on the ship," Cheyenne says.

"You were on the Gillihad 1? I heard that there was a zombie outbreak on that ship," Max says.

"Yeah, zombies. We'll leave it at that."

"Wait, where's your Galactic Fleet insignia?" Max asks.

"I'm not with the Galactic Fleet anymore. Technically. In fact, my whole crew is over there."

Max turns, looking back at a lunch table with two human males, a really cool-looking lizard-type alien female with her long, black hair in box braids, and a female android who has her arm open as she repairs herself. They look like a rag-tag team of salvagers.

"We just stopped by to throw my buddy John here a good luck party. If you wanna come, too, it's tonight at 2000 hours in the party room," Cheyenne says.

"What? Yes, please. One, I love a good party. Two, that's John Lewis!" Max says with wide eyes and admiration. "He's like the most OG mixed martial artist there is!"

"Okay, buddy. Calm down. You're nerding out. Also, call me Orion. No one knows me as Cheyenne, not in a long time. Well, we'll see you tonight, then," Orion says, walking away.

Max turns back, looking at the table where his crew is sitting. They look like homeless people. The fat male human looks similar to Max. They wave to each other. Then, as if synergistically, they both reach into their hoodie pockets, pulling out a Twinkie. Noticing this, they air high-five with the snack cake and take a bite.

CHAPTER 8

Robbie stands in front of a large shed attached to a dock on a private beach that is hidden away from the general public. His eyes are closed and he is breathing in the sea air. He loves the smell of the salt and sea. He can feel the sun's rays warming his head. He opens his eyes, smiling wide, and walks to the door of the rust-stained metal shed, opening it.

Walking inside, he flips the large power lever mounted on the wall to his right. The inconspicuous shed is far more state-of-the-art than it looks. Four jet skis sit on risers out of the water. They are blue with white pin stripping and on the bow sits the Team Adventure Club logo, bright and proud. The power flickers on, revealing a complete computer station with dual monitors and an elaborate satellite array that finishes booting up and then comes to life. On the outside of the shed, a large dish pops up and starts moving.

Robbie rushes over to the monitors and keyboard, typing in his special code to activate the computer.

"W. Seven. Money symbol. Money symbol. F. X. Percent sign. Ampersand. Zero. One.

B.L.A.**K.E.," Robbie says under his breath. "Who made this code?"

The shed door swings open as Leanne walks in with Carrie. They seem a little out of breath and frustrated. Carrie drops her large backpack to the floor and immediately pulls out a folding chair from against the wall, sitting down.

"It's too hot out already," Carrie says, plopping down in the seat.

"We had to walk because I keep forgetting my thruster to the scooter is busted. We have to get that fixed," Leanne says.

"Yeah, thanks for waiting," Carrie says sarcastically to Robbie.

Robbie looks over at her with a smirk. "Don't hate this face. I'm adorable."

"Do we look like Deborah Valentine? Your charm and good looks don't work with us, buddy," Leanne says, cocking her head to the side.

"Yes. It does," Robbie says.

"No," Carrie says.

"Look at this smile," Robbie says, grinning ear to ear.

Leanne and Carrie both fold their arms in disapproval.

Robbie's shoulders drop, and he flashes a frown, pretending to be sad. Then his phone chimes several times. He pulls his phone out of his pocket and sees he has a text message. It's from Deborah. He reads it, smiling.

"See, someone thinks I'm cute," Robbie says, holding up the phone up to Carrie and Leanne to show them a picture of Deborah at the beach.

Carrie and Leanne both stick out their tongues like they are vomiting.

"Blah!" they moan in unison.

"Whatever. Leanne, give me that thruster. I'll hold on to it until I can fix it," Robbie says.

Leanne reaches into her satchel, pulling out the large, ten-inch by six-inch thruster, which looks very similar to a jet engine, handing it to Robbie, who puts it on the workbench underneath the array of monitors. She hands him the second one. He puts it next to the first one. He can see on the exterior sides there are traces of black smoke and pauses for a moment, looking at the jet skis, then back at the thrusters.

"Let's go! I'll fix them once we get to the island," Robbie says, scooping the thrusters into his backpack.

"Ah, good. Nice and heavy," Robbie says sarcastically.

Walking over to the large switch panel mounted on the wall by the door, Robbie pulls the first lever and the first jet ski starts to lower into the water.

Carrie walks over to a mounted locker system that has five large locker doors. She opens the locker that has her nameplate at the top. Pulling out a wet suit, she puts it on over her swimsuit, zipping it up. The suit is light blue and white with accents and bright green pin striping along the seams. She then puts on a bright orange form-fitting life preserver vest. The back of the vest has the letters T.A.C. in thick black letters across the top center. She pulls out a pair of aquatic shoes that are the same blue as her suit, putting them on.

Leanne opens her locker and puts on her wetsuit, which has the same color scheme as Carrie's. She, too, puts on an orange life preserver vest and matching shoes. She waits as the second jet ski lowers to the water before she gets on. Both Carrie and Leanne put on cool, sleek blue and white helmets with a clear face screen.

Robbie lowers the last lever, then goes over to his locker to put on his matching wetsuit, shoes, and vest. He slings his backpack on over the vest, then checks the front pockets of the vest.

"Flare gun and flares? Check. Flashlight? Check. Emergency matches and kindling? Check. Satellite Positioning Monitoring Galactic Communication Device? Check. Team Adventure Club Communicator?" Robbie Says.

"Check!" they all say out loud.

They start their jet skis and head out of the covering of the shed out into Bellview Bay, heading out to sea.

"We will be at the island in about an hour or so. If we don't run into a storm." Robbie says over the TAC-COM.

"If we run into a storm, we'll probably die," Leanne says.

"No sir. These have been upgraded with submarine technology. There's a red button on the left handle. Press that and a bubble shield pops up and over the entire jet ski and we can go fully submersible for up to an hour. And fifty feet deep. We can out-dive any storm," Robbie says.

"That's rad!" Carrie says.

The jet skis race across the vast open ocean as the white clouds span across the clear visors like a video screen. Leanne sits comfortably on her craft, staring off into the distance in amazement at the blue of the sky. She and Carrie make eye contact, giving each other the thumbs up when a pod of dolphins pops up between them. The dolphins are gray and white and seem very playful as they dip in and out of the water, riding the small waves the jet skis make. Carrie and Leanne start doing a crisscross pattern, jumping over each other's wake as the dolphins jump over the crossing wake's diamond-shaped middle. Soon the dolphins leave. Robbie watches as the dolphins swim off and now the three of them are sad.

"Bye, dolphins," Carrie says with a frown.

"We love you. Come back and see us," Leanne says.

Robbie sniffles a little.

"Are you crying?" Carrie asks.

"What? Yes. That was a magical moment. I'm allowed to cry," Robbie says.

"Yeah. Cry it out, fella," Leanne says.

CHAPTER 9

The rock face of the cave is slippery from the ocean water and various vegetation that grows vigorously throughout the entire island. Jaxx, who is tall and thin, reaches up to a rocky platform, pulls himself up to the ledge, then spins around to grab his recon partner, lifting him up onto the same ledge.

"Easy does it. This stuff is slipperier than bacon grease on a railroad track," he says.

Junior grunts as he gains his footing. They look out before them and see more rocky surfaces and a large cave. The volcanic rock looks alien to them as they traverse over it.

"I feel like we're on another planet," Junior says.

Jaxx holds up a square handheld GPS device that has a small screen with dials on both sides of it. There is a green radar that shows the direction they need to go. Jaxx flips the dial on the top right of the device and the screen switches to a satellite view of their exact location. Jaxx looks around for a landmark to match their location and sees the same peak of one of the rocky crests as on the viewfinder.

"Yep, we're on track. This way through the cave," he says.

They continue on their path into the dark cave. They both touch a button on the side of their helmets and a bright spotlight turns on, illuminating the cave walls. The cave is long and dark. Water drips off the top of the cave walls. Huge multicolored stalagmites and stalactites fill up the cave, making some areas hard to get through. The wet terrain is beautiful and deadly.

Far on the other side of the island, Mike and Scott are battling a completely different type of terrain. They are skirting around the rocky cliffs that border a large, majestic lagoon. They reach a steep, slick, smooth cliff face. Mike pulls out his GPS device looking at it. He seems confused for a moment.

"What's wrong?" Scott asks.

Mike shows the device to Scott, and he watches the screen suffer from interference as it goes from static, to numbers, to the radar, and back again.

"Aren't these things like 50,000 bucks?" Scott asks.

"67,000, actually. And yeah, it'd be nice if they worked properly. Ready your grappling hook and let's go up to the ledge and around. We need to get over there to that large dark spot on the side of the cliff wall," Mike says.

"That looks like a cave," Scott says.

"Well, we would know if our equipment worked right. I love working in the private sector," Mike says.

They pull a rifle-like weapon from their backpacks and then attach a metal hook with a nylon rope. They aim the weapon toward the cliff thirty feet above them and fire. The grappling hook slams into the rock and secures itself by sheer force. They clip the rifle to their belts, activating the device. They are hoisted up with ease and make it to the new ledge without incident.

Once they stabilize themselves, they release the metal hook from the rope and place it back into their packs, then hitting a button, the rope retracts automatically. They put the rifle back into their packs as well. They continue on their path to the dark spot about three hundred yards away from them. The view from where they are is like something out of *Peter Pan*. The high rock faces and the crystal-clear lagoon, palm trees, and black sand create a luxurious location.

"Well, I know where I'm moving when I retire," Mike says.

Back at the helicopter, Gretchen sits with Jacob as they continued their conversation about video games.

"Of course, you can't go into the sulfur mines of Modax without a rebreather! What was I thinking?" she asks.

"Yeah, well, I almost had a golden run gem, but at the very last second, I got blown up by a glitter bomb. I haven't touched *Clown Town* since," Jacob says.

"Oh, I've rage-quit a few times myself," Gretchen says.

"You know, I haven't heard from the team in a hot minute. Raven One to recon team, over," he says.

The radio sits silent. Jacob adjusts his communication dials and tries again. "Raven One to recon team, over," he says.

Still nothing. Jacob stares into the lagoon from high above. He taps the side of his visor and the color spectrum changes to green. Still nothing. He taps it again and the color changes to purple. That's when he sees a pod of whales swimming in the lagoon.

"Wait, what?" he asks.

"What is it?" Gretchen says.

"There is a pod of humpback whales inside the lagoon," he says.

"Isn't this an inactive volcano? And that's a lagoon. There's no way in by sea," she says.

"Exactly. There must be another way in somewhere. Maybe underwater. Look down there and tap your visor twice and you'll see them," he says.

Gretchen leans over, looking out the front of the helicopter windshield, spotting the whales.

"Wow, just wow. Look at them. Awe, there's a baby. This job may be the best one I've ever had!" she exclaims.

"Working for Hedgestone? Give it time. I've never met an assistant twice, if you know what I mean," he says.

"I heard there's a high turnover rate with Hedgestone Inc.," she says.

"Turnover rate? Try early retirement rate," he says.

Meanwhile, far beneath them, Jaxx and Junior are making their way through the dangerous interior of the volcanic caves.

"What are we looking for, exactly?" Junior asks.

"I think it's a part of a shuttle or something. I heard part of a ship. Who knows with Hedgestone and his billion-dollar secrets," Jaxx says.

They can see light toward a part of the cave and head toward it. As they make their way around a ten-foot-wide stalagmite, an open section of the cave, complete with sunlight and an ecosystem, is revealed. There are tall trees and other vegetation, some of which Jaxx and Junior have never seen, like a bright pink and white succulent with spiky palms. There is also an orange type of fruit hanging from a unique set of vines.

"What are these?" Jaxx asks.

"Fruit?" Junior asks.

"I can see it's a fruit of some kind," he says.

"Orange fruit?" Junior asks.

Jaxx plucks one from a vine, ripping it open. The inside is white like a dragon fruit, but there is only one seed, like an avocado.

"Think it's edible?" he asks.

Junior shrugs, picking his own off the vine. "Let's find out."

"Not here. Let's take some with us. Try them back on dry land, near a bathroom and a hospital, just in case," Jaxx says.

"Good idea," Junior says.

Suddenly a rock hits Jaxx's helmet and he and Junior immediately go into defense mode, looking around until they see Mike and Scott standing above them high on a ledge, looking into the atrium of sorts.

"You guys can use your radios, ya know," he says.

The two men don't answer.

"Can you two hear me?" Jaxx asks.

Still nothing. Jaxx waves at them and then points to his helmet.

Mike looks at Scott. "I don't think their mics are working," he says.

"Jaxx? Junior? Can you guys hear us?" Scott asks.

Nothing. They look down at the two men who seem to be arguing over the fruit they are holding.

Scott pops off his helmet and yells. "We can't hear you."

Jaxx and Junior look up at the men taking off their helmets. They yell, "Your comms are broken."

Scott yells back, "No, your comms are broken."

Junior looks at Jaxx. "How does he know our comms are broken? Maybe theirs are broken."

Scott points to a ledge about halfway for both of them. "Go there," he says.

All men nod and start for the ledge. The slick rock doesn't make it easier for any of them. But with skill and luck, they make it. Finally, the men are together again.

"Are your comms broken?" Jaxx asks.

"We thought yours were," Scott says.

"Maybe," Jaxx says.

"Well, I know our GPS device is broken. It's gone all wonky," Scott says.

Jaxx takes out his GPS device, looking at it. It is going haywire, flipping from screen to screen, and the radar just blinks like a strobe light.

"Well, ours was working. It has to be the island's natural magnetic field. Like the Bermuda Triangle," Jaxx says.

"How much farther to our point of interest?" Scott says.

"Well, it should be right—" Jaxx stops mid-sentence when he sees a huge pirate ship, still intact, sitting in the enclosed cove. The men all turn to look in amazement. Their eyes go wide, and, for an instant, they are kids again.

"That's a pirate ship," Junior says.

The men stare in awe at the massive two-mast sailing vessel. It seems quite odd at first, then mind-boggling a second later. The more they study it, the more confused they get. The beautiful, pristine ship has several decks and six portholes on both the upper decks, for a total of twelve portholes on one side. Above that is the main deck that has four cannons sitting in position. The sails are down and stowed, but the men can see that there is fabric still attached. The ship's entirety is 165 feet long.

"That's a pirate ship!" Mike says.

"It sure is," Jaxx says.

"First., how did it get inside a cave on a dead volcano in the middle of the ocean? Two, are we splitting the gold we plunder?" Junior asks.

"Well, one answer is, it's a pirate ship, so it sailed on the ocean. So, that's one answer," Mike says.

The men reach a long stretch of beach that leads them to the loading ramp. The wood looks brand new, and well taken care of.

"Okay. Something's off. This looks like a brand-new ship. I mean, look at the shine on the bow. What's that say?" Junior asks.

"The Blasted Dragon," Scott reads out loud.

Junior thinks for a moment. "That sounds familiar," he says.

The men move closer for a better inspection. They follow the loading ramp to the main deck, still in complete awe. The two masts stand tall before them, almost scraping the ceiling of the enclosed cove. Mike walks up to a cannon, rubbing his hand along it.

"Guys, this feels brand new. Look, no dirt," Mike says, showing his fingers to the team.

"I don't get it. What is happening?" Scott asks.

"I'll tell you. This has Hedgestone written all over it. He's up to something. He never ceases to amaze me. I've done like seven jobs for this dude and every one is completely different. This by far is the coolest one I've been on. Okay, get pictures, and don't touch anything. Then we get out of here," Jaxx says.

Just then, they all hear a loud snarl behind them. They turn around to see a large, red-headed man standing there in full pirate attire. His long coat is dark green with shiny gold buttons on the lapel and cuffs. Across his chest is a dark brown sash that is tied with a gold buckle. Slipped into the sash are two blunderbusses. His dark red shirt underneath has huge ruffles. His dark black and gold petticoat breeches are tied at the knee above his large, black, leather boots. On his side is the sheath for his silver and gold encrusted cutlass. On his other side is a holstered throwing ax. He is massive, at least six and a half feet tall, with long, dirty, red hair, a sunburned face, and a long red beard tied into three braids.

"Who be daring to be trespassin' on The Blasted Dragon?" he asks.

The men look at him as he pushes his blade against Jaxx's throat. The men quickly pull out their side arms but they are no match for Captain Cutthroat.

"Aye, I got guns too, boys," he says, pulling out one of the blunderbusses from his sash.

The men stare at each other in a standoff. Each waiting for the other to make a move. The men are more confused than threatened.

"Are you supposed to be a pirate?" Jaxx asks.

"Aye, boy. I am Woodruff Rutledge, one of the worst pirates you will ever meet. But ye might know me better as Captain Cutthroat," he says.

He smacks the gun out of Mike's hand and into the water. Then he pushes Jaxx back and over the wooden railing of the ship. Jaxx does a backward somersault into the shallow water.

Scott aims his gun at Captain Cutthroat, but the cutlass makes quick work of it and slices it in half. Scott just looks at his gun as it slides apart. Junior tries to tackle Captain Cutthroat, but it's like running headlong into a brick wall. Captain Cutthroat just laughs at the feeble attempt.

Captain Cutthroat picks Junior up, spinning him upside down, and tosses him into the large pool of water below.

"Get off me ship," Captain Cutthroat says.

Mike does a spin kick, hitting the pirate right in his chest, but it doesn't even move him. Captain Cutthroat bashes him on the head with the pommel of the cutlass, knocking him down and splitting his helmet open. Both halves fall off of Mike's head, leaving his head completely exposed.

Captain Cutthroat leans into the man's face. Mike can see all the scars and smell his bad breath.

"Ye best be leaving before I run ya through and feed ya to me pet sharks."

Mike yells in fear. Captain Cutthroat yells back in Mike's face.

"Run, ye scalawags!" he says.

Captain Cutthroat picks up Mike by his collar, holding him up with one hand. He walks him over to the side of the ship and lets him go. Mike falls into the water backwards, then sinks a little.

Captain Cutthroat aims one of the cannons at the water, striking his cutlass against the metal that holds the cannon into place. A spark flies, igniting the cannon's fuse.

"I would swim faster, ye yellow bellies," he says.

The men swim as fast as they can when the cannon fires, blasting a cannonball into the wall with a massive explosion. Scott and Junior are blown out of the water and onto the rocky land. Jaxx is out of the water, rushing to his men.

"You guys alright?" he asks.

Scott and Junior crawl to their knees as Jaxx and Mike help them up.

"Run," Jaxx yells.

"Is he firing cannonballs at us?" Scott asks.

The men stumble over each other as they round the corner of the rocky cave. Mike trips, falling and knocking Jaxx and Junior down with him. They tumble to a stop. Scott slides on his feet, looking back at the men.

"Stop fooling around. We gotta get the hell out of here. We are not prepared for cannon fire!" Scott says.

The men moan, getting to their feet, and take off running again into the dark cave.

CHAPTER 10

Gretchen is all but falling asleep when a thunderous boom knocks her out of her daze. She looks around and then at Jacob.

"What was that?" she asks.

"Sounded like an explosion, but it could have been a cave roof collapsing," he says.

Jacob looks down at his console flipping a red switch and the screen in the middle of the control panel comes to life. It's a radar screen that blips every few seconds, revealing movement.

"Just in case it's something else. This will let us know if something's closer to us than 200 feet," he says.

The radar blips as Gretchen watches it. Then she sees four red dots appear. They are approaching the helicopter quickly.

"You seeing this?" she asks.

"Yep. I bet that's our boys. And man, are they moving," he says.

Jaxx leaps over a gap in the rock, followed by his team. As Mike lands, another explosion happens twenty feet behind him. Dirt and shards of rock pelt the men, covering them.

"Move. Move. Move," Jaxx orders loudly.

Scott sees the helicopter and starts waving, making a whirring motion with his right hand. Their speed is impressive, especially since the terrain is all but unmanageable. The large jagged rocks are surrounded by smaller jagged rocks, but the dangers are the cracks and crevasses. One wrong move and someone can break an ankle or shatter a shin bone or pop a kneecap. It's treacherous to navigate, but for men who are being fired upon by a cannon, this may not be the most stressful situation they have ever been in.

"I hate cannons. You guys know that," Scott says.

"Yes. We know!" Junior says.

Inside the cockpit of the helicopter, Jacob starts pressing buttons and flipping switches. One switch in particular opens both sliding doors on the hull of the helicopter. The loud sliding mechanism clanks into position with a tangy, metallic thud.

"Can you guys hear me?" Jacob asks.

The men keep running. Only fifty yards remain. Mike and Scott power themselves up and run faster. Junior and Jaxx keep pace, monitoring their breath.

"We need to not panic, guys. We've been in worse than this," Jaxx says.

"It's cannon fire. What don't you understand, man?" Scott asks.

Scott reaches the side of the helicopter, leaping in with such force he almost flies right out the other side. Scott kisses the floor, then pulls himself into his seat just as Mike barrels in, landing in his own seat. They lock themselves in, looking out to see Jaxx and Junior run and hop in.

"Are your comms on?" Jacob asks.

"Yeah, wait... Testing?" Jaxx says.

Jaxx looks at his gear and sees that the radio is on. But there is no signal. He shakes his head at Jacob.

"We got to go. Get us in the air. We are under fire," Jaxx says, smacking the roof of the helicopter.

Jacob turns back around and in two moves, the helicopter is up and spinning in the opposite direction.

"What happened out there?" Jacob asks.

"Do you guys need medical attention?" Gretchen asks.

"I don't know what kind of game Hedgestone is playing, but we need to radio him directly to his phone. Now. I need answers," Jaxx says.

Gretchen turns, looking back at Jaxx. Her face shows serious concern.

"What happened down there?" she asks.

"There's a massive pirate ship," Scott says. "With cannons. That work," he continues.

"What? A pirate?" Gretchen asks.

"Yeah, a pirate ship. With a real pirate. Get Hedgestone on the phone now!" Jaxx says.

Gretchen turns back around, pulling out the satellite phone and dialing in the passcode. The phone beeps and a new screen appears. Gretchen dials in a long series of numbers and it starts ringing. Then a weird Muzak-type of melody plays for a moment. Everyone listens to it.

"That's 'Ode to Joy,' but, like, on a keyboard," Mike says.

"Hold for Sir Oliver Hedgestone," an operator says.

"This is Hedgestone. It better be good," Sir Hedgestone says.

"Out of respect, I'll assume you are not playing some kind of weird eccentric billionaire-style *The Most Dangerous Game* and just tell you that, one, we're not happy. Two, there is the biggest, most fabulous pirate ship I've ever seen. And three, said pirate is trying to kill us. That being said, this is not a trick, is it?" Jaxx asks.

"I can assure you that this is not a trick. What exactly did you find?" Sir Hedgestone asks.

"A giant pirate ship and a pirate," Jaxx says.

"Did you get the name of the ship or the pirate?" Sir Hedgestone asks.

"Yeah, something like The Drunk Lizard, no Wasted Lagoon, and his name was Captain Wooley? No... Woody. Wait... Rudy. It was Captain Rudy of The Wasted Macaroon," Jaxx says.

"That sounds incorrect," Sir Hedgestone says.

"It was The Blasted Dragon. And his name is Woodruff Rutledge, and he goes by Captain Cutthroat," Scott says.

Gretchen types all the names into her tablet and starts reading over the pages. Her eyes go wide when she starts to realize who Captain Cutthroat is.

"Wait, there was a dude pretending to be a pirate on a lost pirate ship?" Gretchen asks.

"No, he was real for sure. Mean. Ugly," Junior says.

"Gentleman, I hope you know what you've discovered. This is the find of the century. Go back and get me that ship and all its contents. I will triple your pay starting yesterday. Do not let anyone know what is there. Secure the area at all costs. I will be sending a cargo carrier to your location once you're on site and ping the coordinates to me," Sir Hedgestone says.

"With all due respect, sir, we are not equipped to handle this," Jaxx says.

"The four of you can't take down a pirate?" Sir Hedgestone asks.

The four men looked at each other and nod in various directions. Jaxx breathes heavily and thinks for a minute.

"I don't think we can. He is well armed—"

"With cannons!" Scott interjects.

Jaxx just looks at Scott and shakes his head. "Yes, with cannons and personal armament as well, at least two pistols and one sword, for sure," Jaxx continues.

"You don't have any pistols on you?" Sir Hedgestone asks.

"No, sir," Jaxx says.

"Thankfully, there is a compartment in the floorboard. Open it up. There are weapons in there. Use them and secure that ship, gentlemen. I will have backup in route within ten minutes," Sir Hedgestone says.

"We are now forty minutes away, sir," Jacob says.

"Well, turn your baby bird back around and get those men to that ship," Sir Hedgestone says.

"Yes, sir," Jacob says.

Jacob pulls on the controls and the helicopter slowly tilts to the left as Jacob turns the large executive helicopter back toward the island. As he looks across the vast ocean, he sees that dark clouds are forming off in the distance. He reaches down to his console, pressing a button and the radar switches screens again. This time it's a weather radar. The screen is completely red on the left side. Jacob looks back out his window at the clouds.

"Well, it's gonna get bumpy," Jacob says.

Gretchen looks at the clouds, and the gray clouds split for a brief second as a huge bolt of lightning strikes.

"Do we have to go through that?" Gretchen asks.

"No, we're going to be *in* it. It's headed right toward the island," he says.

"Oh, good." Gretchen sighs.

CHAPTER 11

Team Adventure Club arrives at the south-east corner of the rocky island. The waves are pushing hard now as the storm approaches. Carrie turns her jet ski to the left so she can drift into the shallow shoreline on her right. Leanne runs her jet ski right onto the sandy shore, making an open trench that quickly fills with seawater. The bottom of the vehicle grinds against the coarse, white shells.

Robbie does the same as Leanne and immediately hops off his jet ski. He pulls out his map, which is now laminated, looking at it, then at the rocky structures. He holds the map to the outline of the island, smiling widely. Pulling out his journal, he reads his notes. *Find the mouth of madness.* Robbie looks around. *What does that mean?*

"I wish there was an actual treasure map. These feel more like suggestions," Robbie says.

Carrie walks up, tying a red and white nylon rope to a large rock on the shore. Her hands burn from the coarse, wet rope as she pulls it tight.

"Tie up your jet ski, guys," Carrie says.

Leanne opens the seat compartment of the jet ski, pulling out the exact same colored rope. She ties a knot around the metal cleat. She finds a large rock with a nice groove she can rest the rope in and ties it off.

"All set," Leanne says.

Robbie takes his rope, snaking it through the front cleat of his jet ski and through both Carrie's and Leanne's jet skis, securing them all together. Then he taps his TAC-COM, activating his grappling hook. He shoots it into the side of the cliff face, pulling the cable out ten feet. He takes his cable and secures it to his jet ski. They are now secure.

"These ain't going anywhere," Robbie says.

He opens a case on the side of the jet ski, pulling at a spiraled cable. Opening his TAC-COM, he threads the cable in and attaches another grappling hook, snapping the TAC-COM closed.

"Which way, Robbie?" Carrie asks.

"I'm going to say this way," Robbie says, pointing to the east of them.

Carrie and Leanne both turn looking to the horizon, which is a massive black rock face. The volcano's jagged edges make it seem like an impossible feat to climb.

"Man, I wish we had jet packs," Leanne says.

"We can't just fly all over in jet packs all the time. Someone will notice," Carrie says.

"When is Uncle Max getting back?" Robbie asks.

"Not for, like, three weeks, apparently," Leanne says.

Carrie starts walking toward where Robbie pointed, the rocks grinding beneath her feet. Carrie reaches an access point to what looks like a path. She follows the path with her eyes, seeing that it goes far up the side of the mountain.

"There's a path over here. I think it's a path," Carrie says.

"As good as any, I guess," Robbie says.

"Have you two lost your brains?" Leanne asks.

Leanne points her left arm at the side of the steep cliff, and with her other hand, she taps on her TAC-COM. The digital screen lights up with what looks like a pie chart but is just the degree of angle at which she needs to fire her grappling hook. She fires the mechanism and the hook slams into the rock twenty feet above her. She gives them a side smirk and zips up the mountain. Landing her feet perfectly, she turns to look down at them.

"Let's go!" she says.

Robbie and Carrie both give big sighs and then aim their TAC-COM, firing their grappling hooks up the side of the mountain face. Within two seconds, they are next to Leanne. They find footing and fire again. They leap another twenty feet up the side of the mountain. Again, they find footing and launch, climbing another twenty feet. Carrie looks down beneath them and sees they are now sixty feet up the mountain. They fire again, moving another twenty feet upward. Robbie sees a plateau that levels off and takes a break for a moment. He plops on the rock, slinging his backpack around to the front as he unzips the front small pocket, pulling out a granola bar.

"Anyone hungry?" Robbie asks.

Carrie walks up, sticking out her hand, and Robbie puts a chocolate bar in it. She rips the package open and crams the bar in her mouth, taking a big bite. Her attention is taken by something off in the distance. She can see the large black clouds forming a massive storm. She taps on her TAC-COM until a radio wave signal is found, then she scans for an incoming signal. Her TAC-COM comes to life with a female voice. "Seacraft advisory for all ships. Tropical storm Marietta is producing waves over fifteen feet high, and winds at sixty-five knots out of the east. Three-foot surge for all coastal communities. Please stay off the seas until 8 p.m. tonight. You're listening to Jessica Shear of the Red Lighthouse. Now back to Kenny Goodwind and the Magic Harps."

"What are knots, anyway? Why can't they just say, like, miles per hour?" Robbie asks.

"Knots is... are? Is. Knots is the measurement of speed on the water. It's *knot* the same. See what I did there?" Carrie asks.

"Knots are equal to the speed of nautical miles. Speed is not the same on land. So sixty knots is like seventy miles an hour," Leanne says.

"Robbie, you should know this. Why, with all your pirate knowledge," Carrie says.

"I like pirates. I don't know what you two are talking about," Robbie says.

"Measurements, doink head. Knots were used by sailors, or pirates, as a unit of measurement.

It's to measure the speed of a ship. They would take their chip logs and tie them off every 14.3 meters," Carrie says.

"Okay, what is that in feet?"

"Forty-seven feet," Leanne says.

"Okay, but, more importantly, there's a tropical storm coming. That's going to be very bad for us. We need to find shelter, and fast," Carrie says.

Leanne pulls herself up over a ledge, looking into the vast lagoon that lays out before them a mile down the other side of the mountain. Carrie and Robbie walk up to the ledge, joining her. Carrie is in awe as she looks down into the beautiful blue waters.

"Look over there! A cave. Let's get to that and set up camp. We need to wait out the storm."

Leanne and Robbie both nod their heads.

"Let's move," Carrie says.

The three of them aim their TAC-COMs at a nearby ledge below them and fire. Leanne jumps first, swinging out below them to another ledge. She lands safely, retracting her grappling hook. Carrie swings down, feeling the cool breeze in her hair. The salty air seems a little strong. She can feel her skin tightening and taste the salt on her lips. She lands next to Leanne. Losing their balance, they fall to their butts on the ground, laughing. Robbie lands right next to them as his grappling hook whips back into the TAC-COM. Reaching out his hands, he helps them up to their feet. A strong breeze hits them and it's considerably cooler than before.

"Temperature's dropping. We need to move," Carrie says.

The path before them is narrow but not too steep. They jog as fast as they can without endangering their own lives. Robbie is a little more ambitious and starts leaping over the larger rocks until he lands on a grouping of loose lava rocks. His foot slips, landing him on his back. He starts to slide down the narrow path on his back. Carrie and Leanne stop for a moment, watching him slide down the mountain. Then he is gone and out of sight. They hear his screams as they seem to fade away, followed by a huge splash.

They rush down the pathway to reveal a fallen edge of the cliff that has broken away, creating a drop-off of over ninety feet. Carrie and Leanne look at each other.

"Jump in. It's awesome," Robbie says.

Carrie and Leanne smile and leap off the edge. They soar, holding hands until they crash into the crystal-clear water below. Carrie waits until the very last second, pausing underwater to let the bubbles settle. Then she opens her eyes and looks around. The view is magnificent. Beautifully colored fish swim playfully. She can see schools of wrasses, blue and yellow fish with bits of electric green on their fins and tail. Spinning around, she sees several of the wide-bodied regal blue tangs, with black stripes down the sides of their bodies and bright yellow triangles on their tails, swimming about. Then she sees her favorite fish, the Moorish idol, a very beautiful white, black, and yellow fish with a long snout. Carrie especially loves the elongated dorsal fin and philomantis extension that looks like a whip hanging off the back. Carrie rushes back to the surface before she loses all her air completely. She breaches like a whale gasping for air.

"I literally thought you were dead," Leanne says, floating in the water next to her.

"Did you see all the fish!?" Carrie exclaims.

"Yeah, we're in the ocean," Leanne says.

They swim over to a shoreline where Robbie is ringing out his button-down shirt. His backpack is sitting in the sun, or what sky isn't covered in dark clouds.

"That storm is approaching quick. We should get into this cave and build a fire," Robbie says.

"Good idea," Carrie says.

Leanne is pushing the salt water out of her long hair. She twists it back up into a bun on the back of her head. Then leans over, patting her head, trying to get the water out of her ears. She then opens and closes her mouth, trying to pop her eardrums to no avail. She shakes her head violently back and forth until she's off balance.

"Are you a basset hound?" Carrie asks.

"No, I got water in my right ear," Leanne says.

"Hold your nose and blow," Robbie says.

Leanne holds her nostrils, blowing so hard her eyes almost pop out of her head. She smiles widely, looking at Robbie.

"That worked. Thanks!" She says.

Robbie picks up his backpack, slinging it on his shoulder, and starts walking into the large cave as Carrie and Leanne follow behind him. Robbie stops briefly, pulling out a flare and igniting it. The cave illuminates, revealing just how deep it is. Robbie shrugs, continuing farther into the darkness.

"Oh, this looks safe," Carrie says.

"What could go wrong?" Robbie says.

CHAPTER 12

The ACH160 helicopter shakes as Jacob pilots the entire crew back to the island as they head for the storm directly in front of them. The temperature gauge has dropped ten degrees and the barometer shows there is a significant drop in air pressure. Jacob taps on the screen in the middle of the console, pulling up a radar map. It shows the cloud formation of the oncoming tropical storm.

"Good news is the storm is small. And moving fast. So we can get to the island, then find a spot to hunker down and wait it out. I've seen worse. I've flown through worse," Jacob says.

"Is that supposed to comfort me?" Gretchen asks.

"Not really. It's mainly to comfort me," Jacob says.

The helicopter whirls as the prevailing winds knock it around like a shuttlecock. Jacob holds the joystick firmly in his right hand while his left hand slowly moves the rudder control back and forth as he levels out the massive air machine to counteract the wind shear.

Jaxx and Scott look out the windows and see the approaching storm.

"That looks fun," Jaxx says.

"Did you bring swim floaties?" Scott asks.

The helicopter sways to the left, then dips down to the right, dropping several hundred feet.

"I'm going in low. I found a better spot to land than before. Something more secure," Jacob says.

They fly along the exterior beach coast for a moment, keeping the island on the left side of the helicopter. Mike stares out the window, watching the typical debris go by, most of which is driftwood and clumps of seaweed until Mike sees three jet skis tied together. They fly by so quickly that he tries to pinpoint the location, but he can't find any significant landmarks. *Probably just tourists swimming by the volcano.* Mike looks at his compass, getting a bearing.

"Are there any resorts close by?" Mike asks.

"Nine miles east. The Ka Wai Anuanu. It's a nice place. They have a crystal-clear spring-fed lagoon. It's eighty feet deep. I was there last year for a week. Best time of my life. Why? Going on vacation after this?" Jacob asks.

"Nah. It's nothing," Mike says.

The helicopter turns to the left with a hard bank as it lifts and over a steep rock face. Jacob levels the helicopter as he descends on the other side of the cliff. He scours the edges, looking for a safe place to land, out of the storm. He turns the tail of the helicopter completely around so now they are facing the opposite direction. Gretchen looks for a good spot as the helicopter hovers for a moment.

Jacob pushes the helicopter forward as he passes a clearing that reveals a place that looks like it was made for a helicopter to land. He again spins the tail of the helicopter around and they touch down, going backwards. The low-lying palm tree's fronds flap in the wind and a small dust devil forms as the rotors of the helicopter get closer to the ground. The landing skids sink into the sand as the helicopter touches down safely.

Jacob flips some switches, shutting the helicopter down. He checks all the gauges, making sure everything is working correctly. He then pushes a button on the console and the engine shuts down.

"All clear, guys. Better hustle. That storm isn't going to make it easy," Jacob says.

Mike opens the sliding door on his side as Jaxx opens the sliding door on his side. All four men hop out. Then Mike lifts the passenger seats, and they fold up into a storage area, revealing a large compartment with several black Pelican cases inside.

"Grab a case, gentlemen," Mike says.

Each man grabs a case, then they start making a dash for the cliffs.

"Let's get back to that cave and make our way to that ship. Quietly," Mike says.

"Yeah, no cannons," Scott says.

"Won't matter now. We got weapons," Jaxx says.

The men jog off the beach into the dense jungle of the island. They stop, drop the cases, and kneel next to them as they open them. Mike looks inside his case, pulling out an MK-12

Stunning machine gun. He finds two loaded clips and puts one in the gun, cocking the mechanism back.

Jaxx looks into his case, pulling out a VeriShield wrist bracer and a stun baton. He clicks the bracer on his left arm and, with a twist of his left wrist, a medium-sized vibration shield hums to life.

"This is cool. Throw something at me," Jaxx says.

Junior picks up a large rock, throwing it at the shield. The rock shatters into pieces, covering everyone in dust. They all laugh.

Junior opens his case to reveal six small black grenades. On the side, in yellow letters, they read "Super Bouncy Bomb." Junior opens the paperwork that comes with them. There is a picture diagram of a soldier using the grenade. The pictures are: An outlined drawing of a soldier picking up a Super Bouncy Bomb. Pulling the pin on the Super Bouncy Bomb. Throwing the Super Bouncy Bomb. An enemy in shock as the Super Bouncy Bomb explodes, covering them in a large black inflatable ball as they bounce off into the distance. In big letters, it reads "NON-LETHAL ADVANCED WEAPONS."

Scott opens his case. Looking down, he laughs out loud. Then he pulls out a jet pack. He slings it on, clicking the safety harness together.

"Why do you get a jet pack?" Mike asks.

"It's in my case," Scott says.

"Well, that is, one, simply unfair, and two, not a weapon. How is that going to help against a crazy pirate with cannons?" Mike asks.

"I don't know, but now I have a jet pack. I win," Scott says.

"I have this cool shield and shock baton. Wanna trade?" Jaxx asks.

"Nah, I'll stick with this," Scott says.

"Okay. Whatever. Let's move. Backup will be here shortly and I'd like to have the ship at least secured before they get here," Mike says.

Mike motions for his team to move forward. They jog from the jungle up the entrance to the cave. They stop for a moment when Mike raises his fist.

"Put your night vision contacts in fellas. I almost broke my neck in here last time," Mike says.

Junior, Scott, and Jaxx pull out small, black, rubber contact cases, opening them up. Inside is a right and left contact. They are gray in color. Jaxx leans back, putting in his contacts with ease. Mike almost drops one of his, barely catching it. Scott is holding his eye wide open, trying to put the contact in, but he can't even get close to his eye. Junior crams them into his eyes and then blinks them into place like he's trying to win a blinking contest.

"Someone help him," Mike says, pointing to Scott.

Mike walks over and grabs Scott by the sides of his head, holding it back while Junior holds one of his eyes open and Jaxx puts the contact in. They do this for both eyes. Mike lets go of Scott, who sits up, blinking his eyes as a huge stream of tears runs down his face.

"Thanks," Scott says.

Meanwhile, out on the beach, Jacob gets out of the helicopter to close the pilot's side sliding door, then walks about to the passenger side, shutting that sliding door. He looks up into the sky to see gray and white arcus clouds forming a rolling wavelike crescent of the approaching storm. They are dark and foreboding.

"Well, that's not scary," Jacob says.

He walks back around the helicopter to his door, gets in, and slams the door closed. Gretchen looks out and up through the bubble-shaped front window. She can see the dark clouds approaching.

"Are we safe in here during a tropical storm?" Gretchen asks.

"Nope," Jacob says.

Jacob looks at Gretchen while flipping some switches and powering the helicopter on. The rotor swirls to life, kicking up beach sand. He puts his helmet back on but disconnects the radio transmitter from the headphones. He reaches over to her helmet, pulling out the communications cable.

"We lost signal," Jacob says.

Jacob puts his right hand on the joystick as his left presses buttons under the window to his left. The helicopter whirls to life.

"Wait. We're just leaving them?" Gretchen asks.

"They are to find that ship and secure it. There is a backup team on the way. If you and I stay here, we are going to get caught in the storm. And it will destroy this very nice and very expensive piece of machinery. Along with you and me in it. I'm not running into a gunfight with a bunch of goons. And we can't sit in this and let the storm blow over. However, this is a very fast piece of machinery that can outrun a fifteen-mile-an-hour tropical storm. So buckle up. I've got some fancy flying to do," Jacob says.

"Good plan," Gretchen says.

The helicopter tilts to the right as Jacob skims the skids across the top of the lagoon water for a few moments before he's able to lift the helicopter up a few more feet. He pushes the throttle down and starts to push the vehicle to its limits. He turns left, flying out of the lagoon and up several hundred feet, just over the ridge that separates the two sides of the island with a three-hundred-foot gap.

The helicopter bursts past the arching mountains and back over the sea again. Jacob dips the helicopter down closer to the water and accelerates, the nose of the helicopter dipping down. Jacob looks at the radar, seeing the red clouds increase in distance behind them.

CHAPTER 13

Robbie stops dead in his tracks. He listens for a moment. He scans the darkness, then brings his TAC-COM up, tapping the screen. A main screen opens with rows of icons. Robbie presses the icon that looks like a dinner plate. A small radar map appears on the screen. Robbie motions for the girls to stop walking. He watches as the long, thin hand spins around the circle. Nothing appears. Robbie pushes that screen aside with his finger as the screen goes back to the main set of icons. This time Robbie presses the flashlight button. A large beam of light shines from the end of his TAC-COM.

"I thought I heard a helicopter. So weird," Robbie says.

"No. I thought that, too. But I didn't want to say anything. I mean, I should know what a helicopter sounds like," Leanne says.

Carrie follows Robbie's lead, turning on her flashlight. She is immediately locked in a gaze as she stares at what looks like an inflatable life raft. It's old and covered in cobwebs, mold, and creeping moss. She walks over to the boat that is tied with a rope to a large rock. She follows the path past the inflatable boat that leads to another section of a tunnel. Turning back around, she walks back to the boat, pulling a large green tarp off the back half of the boat.

Leanne and Robbie walk up with their flashlights trained on the boat. They all peer inside and see several German helmets and one folding shovel. Painted in yellow on the back of the shovel, there is the number 66. Carrie leans in over the boat, pulling out a wooden crate about the size of a cooler. The top falls off as she gets it to the side of the boat. The contents of the crate reveal exactly what was going on. Carrie pulls out a black leather-bound book with a hand-drawn map. Everything is written in German, however.

"I can't read this. But I assume they were also looking for gold," Carrie says.

"Are you kidding me? A German World War II boat inside this cave! Of course! Hitler was trying to follow every myth, legend, and historical opportunity he could. He was a loon. And wanted nothing more than to own every piece of art he could find. Gold, silver, and jewels were also on his list," Robbie says.

Carrie hands the map to Robbie, who stares at it for a moment. He pulls out his map to compare them. They are different, but the one thing they have in common is that neither one says where the treasure is.

"I think we're in the right spot. It has to be close. This proves it! A German war boat in here. I am right. Let's go this way," Robbie says.

Robbie starts off down the original tunnel.

"Wait. Why not that way?" Carrie asks.

"Because the boat is pointed this way. Meaning they dragged it this way, for a while it looks like, and continued going down this tunnel. That way. So we should go that way," Robbie says.

"Man, I hope we don't find any dead bodies," Leanne says.

"Yeah, that'd be sick," Robbie says.

"Why did you sound like you wanted to find dead bodies?" Carrie asks.

"What? Who doesn't love dead bodies? Didn't you ever see *Stand By Me?*" Robbie asks.

"Yeah, like a million times," Carrie says. "It's one of my mom's favorite movies."

Carrie's grin grows wide as she stares at Leanne. Her eyes light up and her excitement is becoming too much to contain. Leanne is confused for a moment as she stares at her friend, who now looks like an evil joker who's about to pop. Then she realizes why Carrie is smiling. She's about to break into song. This happens every time Carrie is about to start singing. Her smile goes from ear to ear and her perfect white teeth shine through. Her nose gets all scrunched up, and she starts to giggle. Carrie puts her finger inside her mouth against her cheek. She pulls it out with a pop.

Robbie turns around to see Carrie pop her finger again. Robbie, too, starts to smile and pops his finger as well. He does it again in time with Carrie and they laugh. Robbie starts singing the lollipop song. Carrie joins him on the second line, and by the third, all three kids are singing at the top of their lungs in unison.

They continue to sing and walk down the cave, scanning the area with their flashlights. As they continue farther into the dark cave, they come across more crates. These are even older. Carrie studies the wooden crates that seem very old. There is a stamp on the top of one of the six crates that reads "West India Spice Company, 1790." Carrie opens the crate, and it's empty. She opens another crate, and it, too, is empty.

"Do you think these crates have been here since 1790? That would make them over two hundred years old. Wow, we could come back for these and give them to the Belleview Heights Museum of History," Carrie says.

"And that boat we found. That'd be killer! We'll have to come back next weekend and grab everything. We could load the boat with the crates. If it floats," Robbie says.

They continue down the cave when Robbie is certain he hears something. He stops moving, holding up his right fist. This is the universal sign for hold still. Carrie and Leanne stop in their tracks as they all listen carefully. There is some sort of noise that almost sounds like talking ahead. Robbie shines his flashlight around and sees that there are holes in the walls and ceiling that go all the way through to other cave paths.

"Look, this goes all the way through. That's a cave on the other side. How cool is that?" Robbie asks.

"Shh... I hear talking," Carrie says.

"Wait, we're not the only ones on this island? Weird," Leanne says.

"Is that good or bad?" Carrie asks.

"Why would it be bad?" Robbie asks.

"This is a public island, so I imagine there are people here all the time," Robbie says.

"Oh, yeah. And no one has ever found the treasure or any of this stuff or the boat. I hadn't even heard of this place until you mentioned it, Robbie," Carrie says.

"We'll be okay. What's the worst that could happen?" Robbie asks.

He shines his flashlight down one cave and back to the cave on the other side. He starts walking the way they were going. Carrie and Leanne follow him as the cave starts to have a steep decline. As they walk, they have to lean back a little more with each step.

"Hey, this is starting to really curve. We're going to end up sliding, Robbie," Carrie says.

Robbie stops shining the light down the dark cave. He can see that the grade continues to increase its angle. He lets out a big sigh.

"We might have to go back. I don't want us to get stuck at a steep dead end," Robbie says.

"We'll find another way," Carrie says.

Carrie and Leanne turn around and are about to start moving when a man's face appears before them. He has short, dark hair and is wearing black military fatigues. Behind him are three more men, all dressed like the first man. Carrie notices the patch on his left shoulder. The Hedgestone Inc. logo. She looks back at his face.

"Hedgestone?" Carrie asks.

Jaxx is just as shocked as she is to see not only people but kids down in the cave.

"What are you kids doing down here?" Jaxx asks.

"Run!" Carrie says, turning and knocking Leanne down, and she slides into Robbie. Robbie falls on top of Leanne and they start to slide down the steep cave. Carrie runs after them, then dives to her stomach, sliding with them. They start to pick up speed. They sway back and forth as the rocky floor gives way to slick rock and they really start moving fast. They can barely hold on to each other. The slick floor curves hard to the right and the three of them slide way up on the side of the cave, almost to the ceiling. Then, with a quick swish, they slide to the other side of the cave. They continue to pick up speed. They pass through a subterranean waterfall that soaks them with ice-cold water and really increases their speed. Robbie starts to spin a little, which causes him to kick Carrie in the head, making her spin to her side. Then all of a sudden, silence, as they fell thirty feet to the deep lagoon inside the cave.

The water is pitch black and they can't see anything underwater. Carrie is the first to breach the surface, gasping for air. Panicked, she searches for Leanne and Robbie.

"Guys?" Carrie asks.

Then, with a burst, Robbie pops out of the water, followed by Leanne. They wade in the water and start to laugh. Then they see the huge pirate ship sitting in the back of the cave, lit by a huge ray of sun that is shining in through a naturally formed skylight. Robbie's eyes could not get any bigger if he tried to inflate them with an air pump. He stares in awe at the massive ship sitting crooked on some jagged rocks. The sails are still intact and somehow clean. Then Robbie notices the ship is in very good condition. Carrie is already swimming toward the wooden vessel's rope ladder that is secured to the side.

Leanne dives underwater, popping up next to Carrie as she grabs the rope. Leanne grabs the rope as well. Robbie coasts right up to them and he also grabs the rope.

"Do we go up?" Carrie asks.

"Well, according to sea lore, you cannot board another captain's ship without asking permission to do so," Robbie says.

"Who are we going to ask? The ghost of pirates past?" Carrie asks.

Robbie laughs, then starts up the rope ladder until he reaches the top of the deck, but refrains from going on board.

"Permission to come aboard, Captain?" Robbie asks.

He waits for a moment, almost as if he is expecting an answer, then he hops over the railing to the deck, landing on his feet. His soaking-wet backpack drains water onto the wood. Robbie leans over and grabs Carrie's hand, pulling her up, followed by Leanne. They stand on the deck of the enormous ship with huge smiles.

"Look at the size of this thing!" Robbie says.

"This way bigger than I'd thought it'd be," Leanne says.

"You think those Hedgestone guys followed us?" Carrie asks.

"Hedgestone? Those were Hedgestone men?" Robbie asks.

"Yeah. They looked military for sure," Carrie says.

"Why are they here?" Leanne asks.

"Because they want The Blasted Dragon," Robbie says.

"The what?" Carrie asks.

"The Blasted Dragon. It's the ship you're standing on. That's the name," Robbie says.

"That's a cool name," Leanne says.

Robbie pulls out the laminated map and the book he's been reading. Thankfully, he thought enough to wrap it in plastic. He unwraps the book, thumbs through it to find a picture of Woolworth Rutledge, and holds it up for the girls to see.

"This is the pirate that owned the ship. Woolworth Rutledge aka Captain Cutthroat. One of the most notorious and evil pirates ever to sail the seven seas. It says he killed over 200 men in his day," Robbie says.

"Actually, it's more like 572. But, aye, who's countin'?" Captain Cutthroat says.

Robbie turns to the giant man standing before him. His towering form blocks out the sun as he snarls at the kids. Carrie and Leanne both stare at the man in shock, with their mouths wide open and their eyes bulging out of their heads. Robbie is so close he can smell the leather of his jacket and the salty ocean scent that covers the man. Robbie scans him up and down and is mesmerized by his outfit—the long coat, the ruffled shirt, the loose pants, and all the leather belts. Two blunderbusses on his sash, a long sword on his waist, and long, dreaded, red hair that matches his tri-braided beard. Captain Cutthroat leans over Robbie, Carrie, and Leanne. His breath is horrid and his body odor reeks of sweat and years of seafood.

"Why ye runts be on me ship?" Captain Cutthroat asks.

All three of them scream loudly and in unison. Then, Captain Cutthroat gets hit by three shots that electrocute him. The large pirate stiffens, falling flat on his back. Robbie watches as the pirate shakes and convulses, eventually passing out. Carrie, Robbie, and Leanne all look over the side of the ship to see the four men from before.

"Please get off the ship," Mike says.

The three of them duck down behind the deck's railings, huddling together. They know these men are bad guys. They know they are here for the treasure. They know they have to save the ship and the pirate.

"Okay, these guys are for real," Carrie says.

"Yeah, no duh. They have shock rounds," Leanne says.

"Well, that's better than real rounds or poop rounds," Robbie says.

"Poop rounds?" Carrie asks.

"Yeah, they make you poop. Not good," Robbie says.

Robbie opens his backpack looking inside. He rummages through it but doesn't find anything useful. Some paper, a repair kit for thrusters. Two broken thrusters. One stick of gum. A lighter. Mrs. Tinberbaum's flier for her missing puppy, soaking wet now. Six packages of Pop Tarts, S'mores flavored.

"I got nothing," Robbie says.

"Well, guess we'll have to improvise," Carrie says.

Carrie stands up to address the men, but they are gone. She looks around quickly, but there is no sign of them. She looks straight down the ship's side at the rope ladder, but they are not there either.

"They're gone," Carrie says.

"No, they're not. They are either hiding or are on the ship already," Leanne says.

Carrie sees the door to the captain's quarters. She points at it and starts running for it. Leanne and Robbie follow, leaving the barely awake pirate on the deck floor. Captain Cutthroat can't move his head, but he follows them with his eyes. He can't open his mouth, but he speaks through his teeth.

"Get out of me quarters," Captain Cutthroat says.

They burst into the captain's quarters, slamming the large wooden door closed behind them. It takes all three of them, as the door weighs a lot and is several inches thick. Then they grab the large cast iron latch, slamming it closed, locking them inside.

"Now what?" Leanne asks.

CHAPTER 14

Mike is squatting behind a large rock with his team. The cave is completely silent, causing a moment of eeriness. All they can hear is the water hitting the rocks behind them. Junior peeks over the large rock, looking at The Blasted Dragon.

"There are kids on that ship, and that dude is going to kill them. He shot cannons at us," Scott says.

"Yes, we know. He has cannons. Drop it, Scott. But you're right, we have to get those kids off that ship before something bad happens to them," Mike says.

"Bum rush him. Just attack and take him out," Junior says.

"That doesn't seem like a bad idea. First of all, who the hell is that wannabe pirate? Second, where did these kids come from? And third, let's just get this over with," Jaxx says.

Mike looks over the rock again, noticing there is a wooden ramp that leads up to the stern of the ship above the captain's quarters. Mike motions for Junior and Scott to swim out to the rope ladder while he and Jaxx take the ramp onto the quarterdeck above the captain's quarters. The men nod and make their move. Junior and Scott slowly get into the water, trying not to make a sound, then submerge under the water. Mike and Jaxx sneak over to the wooden ramp, walking up the very steep and very creaky wooden structure to the very top of the quarterdeck. They hop onto the ship as quietly as they can, securing a position behind some large and very old wooden crates.

Meanwhile, in the water, Junior and Scott reach the rope ladder and start to ascend to the main deck of the ship. The water pours off their bodies as they climb, making a lot of noise.

"Can you stop dripping so loudly?" Scott asks.

"We're soaking wet, dummy. What do you want me to do? Dry off first?" Junior asks.

"You're dripping salt water into my eyes," Scott says.

"Close your eyes."

Scott looks up at Junior with a sneer and squinted eyes. He watches as Junior climbs over the wooden railing, putting both his feet on the deck. Then he hears him scream and sees him fly over the railing and back into the water. Then Scott sees the pirate reach over the railing. Grabbing him by the back of his shirt, Captain Cutthroat pulls him high into the air, dangling him over the water, and holds him with one arm, staring him in the face.

"Last warning. Get off me ship, thief," Captain Cutthroat says.

And with a toss, Scott joins his partner in the water. Captain Cutthroat turns to see Mike standing behind him, ready to attack. Captain Cutthroat wastes no time pulling his cutlass. He swings at Mike, who blocks the swing with his MK-12 machine gun. The force of the hit sends Mike backward, and he trips over some wood sticking up off the deck floor. He lands on his back, aiming the gun at Captain Cutthroat, who kicks the gun out of his hands, sending it sliding across the floor, right to Jaxx's feet.

"Get off me ship!" Captain Cutthroat shouts.

Jaxx leaps down, landing between Captain Cutthroat and Mike in a cool superhero pose. Then he rises, activating the VeriShield and pulls out the shock baton.

"Let's do this," Jaxx says.

Captain Cutthroat looks at the shield in awe. He's not quite sure what it is, but he knows that it doesn't matter. He's fought hundreds of men with and without weapons. This one is no different. He steps back, placing his feet into position, extending his sword outward.

"On guard," Captain Cutthroat says.

Jaxx swings the baton, but Captain Cutthroat sidesteps him, slicing his sleeve. He then gets back into fencing position, raising his sword. Jaxx comes at him again and the fierce captain sidesteps him again, stomping on his right foot. Jaxx feels his toes get crushed by the weight of the pirate's boot.

"You are not good at this," Captain Cutthroat says.

Mike has made his way to the machine gun again and checks it for damage. It has a huge scratch down the side of it but seems to be in working order. Mike stands up, aiming his gun at the pirate.

"You're outnumbered, buddy," Mike says.

"Outnumbered by four? Ha! I've been outnumbered by forty. And with better weapons."

Mike stares at the man and realizes he isn't lying. By the time Mike is through his thought, Captain Cutthroat has already leaped into the air, grabbed a rope, and is swinging with both feet at Mike, kicking him in the chest and sending him over the other side of the ship, into much shallower waters. Mike lands in the cold water but hits his lower back on a large rock.

Captain Cutthroat turns his attention back to Jaxx,. who now knows his weapons and skill are no match for the experienced pirate. Captain Cutthroat fakes left then right, throwing his sword at Jaxx. The sword sticks in the rail next to Jaxx. His eyes go wide and he runs to the other side of the deck.

Captain Cutthroat sees the machine gun lying on the deck. He picks it up and examines it, admiring the craftsmanship. He presses a button by the handle and the clip falls out. He catches it looking at the bullets inside.

"That's called a gun," Jaxx says. "And you just emptied it."

"My dear boy, I'm holding three guns on my persons. I have seen many guns in my time. This one is newer. But all guns work the same. Even empty, you can still use it as a weapon," Captain Cutthroat says.

He looks at Jaxx for a moment but then puts the clip back into the gun and racks the slide, loading the chamber.

"Guns, my lad, may have changed in their appearance, but not in their technology," Captain Cutthroat says as he opens fire on Jaxx, who uses the shield to block the onslaught of shock pellets coming at him. Jaxx is cornered. He smiles as he watches Scott climb over the railing, getting back on the ship.

Captain Cutthroat sees Jaxx smile and knows someone is behind him. He's seen this reaction every time someone has thought they had the upper hand. Captain Cutthroat turns around to face Scott head-on as Scott uses the jet pack to boost up into the air and launch a double kick at Captain Cutthroat.

Captain Cutthroat staggers back but doesn't fall as he quickly switches footing to ground himself.

"That is new," Captain Cutthroat says.

Jaxx rushes him from behind, hitting Captain Cutthroat in the back with his shock baton. The surge of electricity brings him to his knees. Jaxx hits him again. But the rugged pirate doesn't fall. He takes the surge again. Jaxx hits him again. And again.

Junior hops over the railing and is now back on the ship. But he is met by the screaming rage of Robbie, who pushes him so hard he flips over the railing back to the water.

Robbie and Captain Cutthroat lock eyes. Scott turns to see Robbie standing there aiming some sort of wrist device at him.

"What are you going to do with that thing, boy?" Scott asks.

"Leave him alone. Take his gold," Robbie says.

Scott feels himself get picked up in a bear hug from behind by Captain Cutthroat, who walks him over to the side of the ship, dropping him over the side, again. Captain Cutthroat turns just in time to see Jaxx rush Robbie, picking him up.

"Let me go!" Robbie says.

"Kid, settle down," Jaxx says.

Robbie looks up to see the huge mast rising off the ship a hundred feet. He aims his TAC-COM at the mast, firing it. The grappling hook slams into the wood and, with a whip, Robbie is pulled from Jaxx's grip and is now high above everyone. Both Jaxx and Captain Cutthroat look up at Robbie.

"I need one of those," they say in unison.

Captain Cutthroat rushes Jaxx, grabbing him by his neck and right knee, and, picking him up over his head, walks him to the edge of the ship and tosses him into the water. Jaxx splashes into the water. Jaxx gasps for air for a moment, then regains his composure.

"We have backup coming. So just sit in your ship, buddy," Jaxx says.

"Run! Before I put your heads on spikes with my other collection of heads," Captain Cutthroat says.

Captain Cutthroat looks up at Robbie, who is now sitting in the crow's nest, about halfway between the deck and the top of the mainmast. Robbie jumps off the mast, then shoots his grappling hook back behind him to the mast again, using it to slow his descent. He lands on the deck in front of Captain Cutthroat.

"You're not afraid of me?" Captain Cutthroat asks.

"No. How are you still alive?" Robbie asks.

The door to the captain's quarters opens as Carrie and Leanne step out. Carrie is holding a large book and reading it aloud.

"Then, in the year of seventeen hundred and forty-eight, I fought off the British royals who were after the gold of King Solomon. I left all thirty men on an island off the coast of Mexico in the Gulf of Mexico. Had it not been for my crew, the fine people of Port Forgua would have never seen their heirlooms or treasure again. The British Empire will have my head for sure if they ever found out that I returned all the treasures they had stolen from those poor farmers," Carrie reads.

Captain Cutthroat retrieves his sword, which is still stuck in his deck railing, putting it back into his scabbard. Carrie continues reading.

"Christmas, eighteen hundred and eleven. I found the missing cross of Saint De Louis, taken by the king of Spain. Three men perished in an unfortunate explosion, caused by said men. I am only doing this to return the gold stolen from those who do not have an army or a navy to protect them. Who, if not myself, will sail these seas, fighting for what is right? The British, the Spanish, and the African kings all fight for gold and jewels and spice and nothing nice. They've killed thousands of innocent people before our eyes. I must continue my work."

"Aye, you found my journal. That's private, lass," Captain Cutthroat says.

Carrie flips through the pages, finding another passage.

"I've been cursed by a Voodoo priest to forever stay on my Blasted Dragon and never to step foot off of her. For if I do, I will surely die. It's been two hundred years, perhaps. So long that I've lost track of the season and time. The last of my friends to die was Cornelius Von Wessen, my first mate and colleague of fifty years. I have been alone for too many years now. Sitting in this cave. The date is nineteen hundred and twenty," Carrie reads.

"You should read this," Robbie says.

Robbie unwraps a small book from plastic as he pulls it out of his backpack handing it to the captain.

"Do I want to?" Captain Cutthroat asks.

"Probably not. The history books say way different," Robbie says.

Leanne has been watching the men as they regroup on the shoreline. They are clearly making another plan of attack. Leanne looks around for a way out, but the only real way out is up through the massive hole in the cave ceiling.

"Guys, they're regrouping," Leanne says.

"Do all of you have those grappling hooks?" Captain Cutthroat asks.

"Yeah, they're our Team Adventure Club communication device. Or I call it TAC-COM for short. It does all kinds of stuff. It's connected to a satellite and to Max, Carrie's uncle," Robbie says.

"What's a satellite?" Captain Cutthroat asks.

"Oh, man, you have so much to catch up on. Do you have a pirate treasure?" Robbie asks.

"Do I? My dear boy, I got a vast stockpile of gold, the likes which ye eyes have yet to see. Folla' me."

CHAPTER 15

Mike is sitting with his team in the dark cave as they contemplate their next move. Mike is squatting next to Jaxx, who keeps peeking up over a large rock, checking to see if the insane Captain Cutthroat is coming after them.

"Mr. Hedgestone, what is the ETA on the second team? We are pinned down here. There is this weird pirate dude who keeps kicking our butts and now some kids showed up," Mike says.

Mike clicks the satellite phone again. "Hello."

Mike hands the phone to Scott. "I'm going back in. We need to secure that ship and help those kids. That monster will probably kill them," Mike says.

"He might kill us," Scott says.

"We know, cannons!" Mike, Junior, and Jaxx say in unison.

Scott's eyes go wide as his teammates all yell at him. He sits down on a nearby rock, folding his arms and sulking. Mike sees his partner is hurting and insulted and walks over to him and sits next to him.

"Hey, big buddy, look. None of us like being shot by cannons. Or anything, for that matter.

Maybe when all this is over, you could go talk to a doctor about your fear of cannons. Tell them all about it. But right now, I need you to focus and help us secure that massive ship full of gold. Because if we don't, Sir Oliver Hedgestone is going to shoot *us* out of a cannon. Okay? So, come on, buddy. One last mission for old time's sake," Mike says, his hand rubbing Scott's shoulder.

Mike stands up smiling, and play-shoves Scott, smacking his head around.

"C'mon big fella, let's go capture a pirate and some gold," Mike says.

Scott nods, smiling and standing up, then hugs Mike.

"You just understand me. I was only eight when Mr. Wiggles was accidentally used as a cannonball and shot into the Grand Canyon. He was my best friend. His cute little nose, and white fluffy fur. Those big ears. Man, he loved carrots. I took him to the Annual Cannonball Championship held every year at the Grand Canyon. See, teams show up to see how far they can shoot cannonballs. Well, Mr. Wiggles hopped away from me and I saw the fat man put him in the cannon. By the time I got there, it was too late. Boom went Mr. Wiggles. He flew so far. And out of sight. I've never had a bunny since. It's been hard," Scott says through his tears. Thick streams of snot pour down his face and chin.

Mike stands there staring at the man who is still grieving thirty years later. Scott falls into him, hugging him tight.

"It was great to talk about it. Let's go get you your pirate. I'll never have Mr. Wiggles back, but I understand that now," Scott says.

He wipes his eyes and scoops his snot off his face, flinging it to the dirt at their feet. Mike looks down at the mucus slung across the rock holding back his vomit.

"That's really gross. How much snot do you have in there?"

"It's from the salt water. It makes me mucusy," Scott says.

Mike walks back over to Junior and Jaxx, who stay silently huddled behind a rock. Mike kneels down next to them.

"I think he's ready," Mike says.

"Did he say his bunny got shot out of a cannon?" Jaxx asks.

Mike nods, then motions for them to stand. As they do, Scott stands there ready.

"Let's go guys. Fight through the pain. We've got some kids to save."

Mike smiles, and the four men start back down the long, dark cave to the lagoon. They round a curve in the water-worn corridor, slowing down. They reach the wide-open lagoon area, taking cover behind a very large black volcanic rock. Its glossiness makes it look like a giant black diamond. Mike leans with his back against it. The cold rock makes him wince and lean forward.

"Well, that's cold," Mike says.

Jaxx peeks around the rock, scanning the ship. He doesn't see the kids or the pirate. He looks around the lagoon cavern, from the natural skylight all the way down to the pool of water that the massive ship sits in.

"I don't see any sign of those kids or that pirate wannabe," Jaxx says.

"I think Hedgestone hired this guy. It's a test. I bet he's got some big mission coming up, and this is a test. Maybe we're, like, the first team to try it," Scott says.

"Why would he put us through a test? We're already some of the best of the best," Mike says.

"That we know of," Scott says.

Mike contemplates the idea for a moment. "Why else would he leave us such a ridiculous array of weapons? These are like prototypes. So, we're testing them out. Fight the pirate, get the gold, get THE JOB," Scott says.

Mike feels bad now, as a soldier should never let his weapon go. And now, Captain Cutthroat has his prototype MK-12 electro-shock rifle, non-lethal, of course. He turns, peering over the rock. The ship is fantastic, and there is no way it's real. So Scott must be right. This is a test with prototypes and there is no way on earth his team is going to fail a test. Now, he finds the motivation to get on that ship, save the kids, and secure the treasure. Oh, and capture the pirate.

"I think you might be right, Scott. This is some kind of skills test. So, let's give them what they want. I did notice the pirate didn't kill us, and we also have non-lethal weapons. This *is* a game. And we're going to win so good. The other teams will have to beat our time," Mike says.

"Wait, this is timed now?" Scott asks.

"What? No. I don't know. Maybe. Let's just go get that gold!" Mike says.

"Is this timed, or is it not timed?" Jaxx asks.

"It's not timed, guys. I said that as, like, if it was timed," Mike says.

"Just get the gold, guys!" Mike says.

Mike leans over the rock, putting his hands to his mouth, cupping his lips.

"Hey, Mr. Pirate Guy! We're coming to get the kids and the gold. So get ready buddy," Mike says.

"Why would you announce that?" Jaxx asks.

"Because this is a game. Who cares if he knows? We just have to beat him. He's literally waiting for us to arrive. That's already begun. And we're losing," Mike says.

"Okay, great! What's the plan?" Scott asks.

"I'm not sure," Mike says.

Mike's satellite phone starts beeping. He fishes it off his belt loop, pressing the large red button on the bottom right of the keypad.

"Hello? Mr. Hedgestone. Yes, three kids. Yes, two girls and a boy. No, there isn't a fat guy with them. No, there's a pirate. A pirate is with them," Mike says.

Mike puts the phone on speaker as Sir Oliver Hedgestone screams over the intercom.

"What pirate?" Hedgestone asks.

"I don't know, sir. There's a pirate on the ship," Mike says.

"Are guys messing with me?" Hedgestone asks.

"No, sir. There's a guy dressed like a pirate on the ship. And three kids," Mike says.

"Is it Team Adventure Club?" Hedgestone asks.

"I don't know what that is, sir," Mike says.

"I bet it's Team Adventure Club. They always ruin my fun. Get those kids away from that so-called pirate and get that gold. We'll be there in thirty minutes, with backup," Hedgestone says.

The phone goes silent. Mike just looks at his team. They know the mission; they know the obstacles. They know they have to win. Mike scans their weapons except his. His is still on The Blasted Dragon, with the so-called pirate. Mike has a plan.

"Okay. Junior, give two of the bouncy bombs to Scott. Scott, jet pack up into the air calling out to the pirate. Hit him with these. They'll bounce him off the ship, then the rest of us can go in and grab the kids and secure the ship. We'll tie everyone up until Hedgestone gets here in thirty," Mike says.

"Look man, I'm not about to get a kidnapping rap by tying up some kids," Scott says.

"Oh, good point. Okay, scare the kids into running away," Mike says.

"That's better," Junior says.

All four men peer up over the large rock, ready for action.

CHAPTER 16

The large double wooden door that leads to the hull of the ship creaks as it opens. Carrie, Leanne, and Robbie stand there as Captain Cutthroat exposes the room with a grand gesture, as if he is presenting guests to an epic suite.

"Behold, my treasure!"

The room is full of chests, crates, barrels, and burlap sacks of gold, silver, jewels, and items made from these precious metals. The table in the middle of the room sits covered in piles of gold jewelry. A beautiful gold ruby-and-emerald-encrusted crown hangs from a gold candelabra. Golden necklaces are piled on top of each other. There is an ornate silver statue of Michael the Archangel. There is a solid gold bull statue and, in the corner, sitting by itself on the hilt of a large silver sword, is a golden helmet with bright gold wings on each side. Centered just above the nose guard and the brow sits one of the largest diamonds Carrie has ever seen.

"That diamond is bigger than the jaguar emerald we found in Africa," Carrie says.

Robbie walks through the treasure, refraining from touching anything. His eyes are so wide they seem as if they will pop out of his head. Leanne finds a golden bowl full of rubies. She digs her hand into the bowl, picking them up and letting the small red gems run through her fingers.

"So this is gold you confiscated from other pirates?" Carrie asks.

"Something like that. I was a young, weak boy. My family had nothing. We were fishermen. My father and I would fish all day, bringing in tons of redfish, mackerel, snook, and just all kinds of crabs and lobster. Knowing what I know now, we ate like kings. But when you're living in the moment, you just hate eating fish and lobster every day. I wanted meat so much. I had heard of steak and potatoes. We didn't have that on my island. There were no cows or donkeys. Then one day, a massive frigate appeared in the early morning and ransacked our village. My father offered them all the fish they could eat. They wanted the gold they heard about in our land. We had no use for gold. It had no value to us. We were fishers and farmers. Gold was useless. You couldn't make weapons from it. And to melt it down was a billion degrees. We let them have it. All of it. And they still beat some of the farmers and my father. He fought two of the men who wanted to take some of the females with them. But my father wouldn't have any of that. They eventually killed him and took what they wanted. I vowed from that day on to find those men and kill them. I never found them. Truth is, I couldn't even remember what they looked like. I knew the captain had dark hair and was English. That's all I could remember.

"I scoured the seas, fighting for the lesser islands. Apparently, several countries didn't like me stealing the gold and jewels they had stolen back. I returned almost all of it. This was my last haul. I took all this back from a Spanish ship that had sailed to a small Mayan island and just decimated them. I found the ship and all its contents.

"In the middle of the fight, a Voodoo priest cursed me to never be able to leave my ship, and, in turn, made me immortal. But if I leave, I die. So, I happened upon this volcano and hid The Blasted Dragon in here for hundreds of years. I've yet but seen a handful of people in that time. Mostly those lost at sea. So, I make them think I'm a spirit and guide them to safety. Been doing that for a hundred years. But you guys are different. And who are those guys? They clearly want my gold," Captain Cutthroat says.

Leanne and Robbie have made themselves comfortable. Robbie has put on the golden helmet with wings and Leanne is sitting inside a huge vase wearing a diamond tiara and has wrapped her hands in gold chains. Carrie, however, is pacing around like a worrywart. She rests her right elbow on her left arm while tapping her right index finger on her chin.

Carrie hears faint yelling that stops her from pacing. She puts her left ear out like a cat. Then she motions for everyone to stop talking. She then tip-toes around, pushing her ear out as far as she can.

"They're yelling at us," Carrie says.

Captain Cutthroat walks over to a circular window, lifting the cover off. Carrie rushes over, putting her ear close to the hole.

"They say they're coming for you, Captain Cutthroat. And they're going to get all the gold," Carrie says.

"Let them try. I've been defending The Blasted Dragon for centuries. Come and bring a lot of guns!" Captain Cutthroat says.

"Oh, no. They have backup coming in twenty minutes. We have to get all of this out of here," Carrie says.

"That's not gonna happen. Unfortunately, my lovely lady isn't seaworthy," Captain Cutthroat says.

Carrie rushes out of the room and up the steep stairs to the main deck. She looks high above her, gauging the opening of the volcano, then looks the entire ship over. The masts. The sails. The bow. The stern.

"Do you have more fabric and/or thread to sew?" Carrie says.

"M'lady, I have plenty of fabric. Every good captain keeps extra linens and sails. A storm could put a wallop on some of the sails. So you'd have to replace them at sea. Well, not me, my crew. Mostly Harvey. He was a good ship-mate. Could sew all kinds of stuff, oh my. I just remembered he made me this for my thirtieth birthday, five hundred years ago. Wow," Captain Cutthroat says.

The suddenly troubled captain sits down on a small barrel. His entire demeanor has changed. He has turned inward now. Contemplative. He stares at the floor. Carrie stops thinking and turns her attention to the sad captain.

"Captain, sir. Are you okay?" Carrie asks.

"What's the point? All this. Maybe it's time to end it. I can fend off the men and you kids can take what you can carry and get out of here. Come back with more people and take it all. You can have it," Captain Cutthroat says.

Robbie jumps up and down in excitement. "We can have it all?" Robbie asks.

"No!" Carrie says. "We are not running away from Hedgestone and his goons, and we certainly are not letting the Fierce Captain Cutthroat die for our sake. No. We are going to craft an air balloon. And it's going to lift us up and out of the volcano. Then we're going to fly it to safety, where we will figure out how to get Woodworth off this vessel and back on dry land," Carrie says.

"What?" everyone else says.

"A hot air balloon," Carrie says.

"I love it," Leanne says.

"I don't understand. What is a hot air balloon?" Captain Cutthroat asks.

Carrie pulls the captain's cutlass out of its scabbard so quickly that even Captain Cutthroat is impressed. She draws a picture of a large round balloon above a horrible depiction of The Blasted Dragon. The captain looks at it for a moment.

"This could work," Captain Cutthroat says.

Captain Cutthroat rushes away. "I'll be right back."

"Leanne, we have to get all those sails down and sew them together to make the balloon. And then somehow get it to lift," Carrie says.

"Leave that to me!" Robbie says.

He flings his backpack off, pulling out the busted thrusters from the scooters. He then pulls out a tool kit from his belt pouch and gets to work taking out a long wire connected to the TAC-COM, connecting it to a port in the thruster.

Leanne has already started up the mast for the first yardarm. She sees that the rope through the sails is a very intricate mechanism that she doesn't quite understand. She moves to the crow's nest, trying to study the entire sail system.

"How does this work?" Leanne asks.

Carrie looks up, yelling back. "I don't know."

"We'll use these. Keep the sails lowered. We'll need them for forward motion with the wind," Captain Cutthroat says.

Captain Cutthroat stands there holding a large stack of fabric in one arm and a crate full of fabric behind him with his other hand. He drops the loose stack to the deck floor.

"I don't know how long it's going to take to sew a fifty-foot balloon, but I'm going to assume longer than twenty minutes," Carrie says.

"Carrie, inside our TAC-COMs, we have sealant that'll hold steel together," Robbie says.

Carrie's eyes light up. She opens her TAC-COM to the internet, pulling up designs for a hot air balloon. After scrolling through a few pictures of cute animal designs, she settles on a regular, good old-fashioned balloon shape. She shows it to Captain Cutthroat. "We need to make that," she says.

Captain Cutthroat flips open a huge square section of fabric. Using his sword, he cuts through the fabric with ease.

"I really like that device. I realize there is much for me to learn out there," Captain Cutthroat says.

"Don't worry about that now. Let's just get this ship and its contents away from these men. I'm sure Sir Oliver Hedgestone will be here soon," Carrie says.

"Sir Oliver Hedgestone? Of the British Hedgestone Foundation?" Captain Cutthroat says.

"British Hedgestone Foundation? I haven't heard of that. But probably. He's a real tyrant. Goes after everything. Art. Gold. Artifacts. You name it. We've been fortunate enough to stop him a few times before he stole something. A giant ruby comes to mind. He's not a nice guy," Carrie says.

Leanne lands next to her. "Man, I was way up there," she says.

The loud chirping that Carrie's, Leanne's, and Robbie's TAC-COMs start making scares them all. Robbie looks at his screen and it is flashing red with the word "INCOMING" on the screen. He looks up to see the small black hand grenade arching toward them. With quick thinking, he anticipates the grenade's landing location and dives toward it. As he slides on his knees, he takes off the golden helmet with wings, slamming it over the projectile.

The Super Bouncy Bomb explodes, causing a large rubber ball to expand instantly. The rubber ball blasts Robbie and his helmet two hundred feet into the air and out of the skylight of the volcano. Robbie soars through the air so quickly he can hardly keep his eyes open. His lips flap like a basset hound with its head out the car window. Finally, Robbie reaches the apex and stops flying, pausing long enough to look to his left and see the massive tropical storm in all its fury. Robbie screams. Then he looks down and screams again. Then he screams as he starts to fall.

Below him, Captain Cutthroat punctures the rubber ball, popping it. Which sends him, Leanne, and Carrie all slamming into crates and barrels. As Robbie falls, he reaches out for his golden helmet, barely touching it with his fingertips, but he grabs it. He realizes he only has seconds as he descends through the skylight of the cave. He looks down at the mast of the ship firing his grappling hook. It's a direct hit. Robbie swings around the mast like a tether ball and lands perfectly on his feet in front of Captain Cutthroat.

"Aye, I think I found my new first mate," the captain says.

"What was that thing?" Carrie asks.

"I don't know. Some new non-lethal grenade? Man, that was intense. Also, the storm is here," Robbie says.

Captain Cutthroat rushes to the cannon sitting on the deck, opening the back of the cannon and shoving a cannonball inside. He packs the gunpowder in and, with the use of his sword and dagger from his belt, he aims a spark directly at the fuse, lighting it. Carrie's eyes go wide. Leanne's eyes go wide. Robbie's eyes go wide. Then boom. The cannonball flies across the interior of the volcano, blasting the ceiling and causing debris to rain down on Mike and his team.

"That'll shut 'em up. Let's move," Captain Cutthroat says.

Carrie lays out more fabric with the help of Leanne. Captain Cutthroat cuts it with his sword. Robbie tinkers with the thrusters as fast as he can. He sticks a thin screwdriver inside the open compartment where the circuitry is. Then he pulls out a portable soldering iron, connecting two wires together. He taps on his TAC-COM, waiting for a diagnosis. The loading circle pauses for a moment. Robbie furrows his brow, hoping this fixes the problem. Then the screen turns green and the thruster's charging light comes on.

"Yes! I did it," Robbie says. "I got the thrusters working. We can put them under the balloon to give us the upthrust. How's that balloon coming?"

"All the fabric is cut. We just need to glue it together. Sewing will take too long," Carrie says.

"Line them up," Leanne says.

All of them lay the fabric out on the deck of the ship in the pattern Carrie shows them.

"Okay, we have to glue along these seams, and hopefully it'll work," Carrie says.

Robbie crawls on all fours to one of the large seams, aiming his TAC-COM at it. He sprays the sealant on the fabric as Carrie pushes the two pieces together. They follow the length of the fabric to the end. Leanne and Captain Cutthroat do the same thing on another piece. They have eight large, curved pieces to fold together. They make quick work of it and soon they are done.

The entire balloon has been fabricated. It's massive, spreading a hundred feet at its widest.

They take large sections of rope tying two pieces to the bow, two pieces to the stern, and two on each side of the ship. They now have six long pieces of thick rope secured to the ship. With what little sealant they have left, they seal the rope to the outside of the balloon, making The Blasted Dragon the basket of the hot air balloon.

"Well, let's see if this works," Captain Cutthroat says.

Robbie has put the two thrusters on the top yardarm facing up. Then Captain Cutthroat and Carrie climb up to him. They grab a piece of the rope attached to the balloon, holding on tight.

"Okay, just drop and it'll drag the balloon over the mast," Captain Cutthroat says.

Carrie and the Captain drop off the yardarm and the weight distribution gives them a slow descent to the deck floor. The balloon is hoisted up and over, covering Robbie as he sits in the crow's nest. Robbie can taste the fibers of the old fabric. He flicks his tongue, spitting as he covers his eyes.

"Oh gross, smells like my dad's socks," Robbie says.

The balloon is in place now. Captain Cutthroat, Carrie, and Leanne wait on Robbie's signal.

Robbie does one last look over the thrusters, waiting for a final charge. The batteries are only at thirty-five percent. Robbie secures his TAC-COM to the crow's nest, then takes the ladder down to the deck, meeting the others.

"We have to wait. The thrusters are not fully charged. Maybe ten minutes."

"Well, that's not going to work. Hedgestone's men will be here in five. We might have to risk it and just go," Carrie says.

Captain Cutthroat walks over to one of his cannons, loading it. He looks out over the vastness of the interior lagoon, hanging his head. He pats the railing of the ship as if he's talking to himself. Standing up, he aims the cannon up a little and to the right.

"They'll never get in once I fire this. It'll collapse the entrance. You'll also run the risk of not being able to leave," Captain Cutthroat says.

"Fire it. We're getting out of here," Carrie says.

The fire sparks and the fuse lights. The slow burn seems to take forever, then the cannon roars to life, exploding and sending a large cannonball into the ceiling just above the entrance they came through a few hours ago. The rock explodes into thousands of pieces, crumbling the entrance. Whoever is on the other side will never get in. Not without dynamite and a bulldozer.

"It is done. Time to face the future," Captain Cutthroat says.

Robbie climbs up the mast to the crow's nest again. He secures himself in by tying a large piece of rope to himself. He checks the TAC-COM, and it reads seventy-five percent. He unlocks his TAC-COM from the mast and puts it back on his wrist. He sits down inside the basket of the crow's nest as he swipes his screen to the ignite icon. He presses the button and the thrusters start.

The loud roar of the thrusters gets the attention of Carrie, Captain Cutthroat, and Leanne, and they all look up and stare. They watch as the large balloon slowly inflates, and keeps inflating, and inflating, and inflating until finally there is a massive balloon hovering over the entire Blasted Dragon.

Captain Cutthroat cannot believe his eyes. Inspired by the moment, he weeps.

"It's like Jules Verne," he says.

"You've read Jules Verne?" Carrie asks.

"I've over a hundred books. I had to teach myself to read better, but I managed and eventually got there. Reading is tough. I got lucky. At some point, a bunch of soldiers showed up with artwork, books, and some relics. They tried to fight me, but I chased them out of here. I think they even left their little boat in a cave tunnel," Captain Cutthroat says.

"I think we saw that. Those were Nazis. Real bad guys," Carrie says.

"Well, I have all the stuff they stole in the treasure room," he says.

The ship suddenly rocks and starts swaying. Captain Cutthroat looks up to see the balloon in its full glory. Robbie is working the thrusters, slowly releasing blasts of fire. The ship lifts out of the water and slowly rises toward the sky. Captain Cutthroat and Carrie rush to the side of the ship, looking over the rails. They are about ten feet out of the water.

"I can't believe this is working," Captain Cutthroat says.

"Let's get it out of here and safely on land. Then we'll say it worked," Carrie says.

The ship continues to rise higher and higher, to everyone's disbelief. They are at least a hundred feet in the air now, closing in on the skylight of the volcano. The water pours off the bottom of the ship, making a sound like it is raining inside the cave itself. As the balloon crests into the open air, it is rocked by wind shear, pushing the entire ship backward.

The stern of the ship slams into the partial ceiling of the cave, smashing the window to the captain's quarters. Then the ship lunges forward, completely smashing the bowsprit, snapping it off. It falls to the water far below them.

The Blasted Dragon finally rises out of the skylight, revealing just how huge it is. The majestic ship floats in the air above the volcano it has been nestled in for over two hundred years. Being in the sunlight again seems to bring life into the ship itself. Robbie sits in the crow's nest watching as the ship is about to take on a tropical storm headlong.

Captain Cutthroat moves to the helm and starts shouting orders. "Carrie, unleash the main sail. There, that rope. Untie it and let it loose. It'll drop the square sail. Leanne, do the same for the foremast. We have to skirt the outside of the storm."

Carrie rushes over to the mast, releasing the large sail. It rises quickly once the wind catches it and the ship thrusts forward with great intention. Carrie falls backward to her butt, sliding into a large crate. Leanne releases the front sails and is knocked off the forecastle, stumbling and slamming into the main deck on her back. She watches as the sails rise and take on wind.

The ship accelerates forward, heading into the storm. Captain Cutthroat spins the steering wheel, trying to get on the outside of the storm.

"Hold tight," he says.

The Blasted Dragon goes headlong into the edge of the storm and the rain starts to pound them. It's hard, and it's cold. Robbie peers over the basket of the crow's nest with fear in his eyes.

CHAPTER 17

The cave crumbles around the men as they move swiftly through the cave tunnels. Mike dives just in time as the cave behind them collapses, completely blocking the entrance to the massive pirate ship. Jaxx rolls to his back, moaning in pain. Junior lays face down, completely covered in so much black dirt he looks like part of the ground and Scott sits in the corner rocking back and forth with his arms crossed in front of his chest.

"Cannons. Why cannons?" Scott says.

Mike stands up, brushing himself off. He walked over to Jaxx, who lies on the ground holding his knee, groaning. Mike helps him up to his feet. Jaxx stretches out his leg, popping his knee with a loud crack and a sigh of relief.

"Was that your knee?" Mike asks.

"I hope so," Jaxx says.

Mike makes a spinning motion with his finger as he whistles and starts hustling down the long, narrow cave. Jaxx limps behind him, as does Scott, who whimpers like a child. Junior, on the other hand, slowly pries himself from the ground and the ten pounds of dirt on his back rolls off as he stands up. He shakes his head and a pound of dirt flies out of his hair. He then shakes his body like a dog flinging dirt off his body. He slowly takes off after them.

Mike is at a steady jog as he makes his way through the maze of cave tunnels. Coming to an intersection, he spots the inflatable boat Team Adventure Club saw earlier. He walks over to it, pulling the tarp off of it. He sees that it has the German flag on it. Then he sees the trench shovel and the M35 *Stahlhelm* with the yellow, black, and orange flag on the side. He takes a step back, looking at the boat again.

"What year is this from?" Mike asks.

Scott and Jaxx jog up to him and they, too, look at the boat.

"That's interesting. Is that a German boat from World War II?" Jaxx asks.

"I think it might be," Mike says.

"It was put here by Hedgestone. I'm telling you. It's all part of the game. And he's a history buff, so it makes total since he'd do that," Jaxx says.

"I guess," Mike says.

Mike starts jogging again, heading out of the cave. As he exits the cave system, he comes out on a shoreline. His eyes burn from the bright sun. He shuts his eyes and takes out the night vision contacts. Jaxx jogs out behind him and shuts his eyes as fast as he can, tripping over rock and slamming his bad knee to the ground. Scott runs out after him and shuts his eyes. But he trips over Jaxx and he, too, falls to the ground.

"Night vision. Night vision," Jaxx says, taking his contacts out.

Scott lays in the sand with his head in his hands. Mike shakes his head and is able to open his eyes, looking around. He doesn't recognize the location. Junior walks out of the cave, putting his contacts back into their rubberized case. He looks at Scott and Jaxx on the ground.

"What are they doing?" Junior asks.

"We're taking a nap," Jaxx says.

Junior helps Jaxx to his feet. Jaxx brushes the sand off of him and he helps Scott up. Junior looks around, confused.

"This isn't where we entered from," Junior says.

"Yeah, I know," Mike says.

Mike looks up to see the dark clouds looming overhead. Then, as if the heavens opened up, rain crashes down on them like someone left the bathtub faucet on full blast. Mike pulls out his walkie-talkie, radioing to Jacob.

"Jacob, we need a recon pick up," Mike says.

"Where's your backup? I had to pull out due to the storm. It was unsafe for the helicopter and its passengers. Looks like you're on a 'hold tight' for now, buddy," Jacob says.

"Okay, thanks. Well, guess we wait here for backup," Mike says.

"They should be here in a minute, I would assume. We need to drop in through the skylight in the cave and get the ship secured," Scott says.

"That's a great idea. We can come in from the top," Mike says.

As he looks up to scan the mountainside and sees The Blasted Dragon soar over them like an airship. The hull of the ship is snapping palm trees as it skims the top of the tree line. The men run and dive for cover as large sections of the huge trees crash all around them.

Mike rolls to his back and watches as the ship soars past them, trying to outrun the storm. Mike gets up, running over to Scott.

"Give me your jet pack," Mike says.

Mike puts the jet pack on almost as quickly as Scott slings it off.

"Junior, give me two of those Super Bouncy Bombs," Mike says.

Mike runs past Junior as he hands him two grenades and, in a hop and a leap, Mike takes off flying the jet pack. The engine roars as Mike rises up past the tops of the palm trees. He is headed straight for the ship. Mike can feel the rain slamming into him like tiny pins of glass stinging his skin. His face is being pelted by the rain and he can barely see where he is going.

Mike pushes the jet pack to its limits, and he touches the hull as he steadies the rocket on his back. He reaches out, trying to grab one of the portholes in the center of the ship. He pulls himself up the side of the ship with the jet pack pushing him up the whole way. Grabbing the side rail to the deck, Mike leaps on board the ship, landing on the deck.

Looking around, he sees that Captain Cutthroat is at the helm. Carrie is standing next to him. He doesn't see Leanne or Robbie. Mike runs and slides to a spot behind a crate. He readies a Super Bouncy Bomb in one hand and as just as he is about to throw it, Leanne grabs his hand, making him drop the Super Bouncy Bomb.

The bomb explodes, and the giant rubber ball expands, hitting Leanne and Mike. Leanne is shot up into the air past the crow's nest, through the interior of the hot air balloon, and high into the storm. Mike is shot off the boat sideways. He tries to use the jet pack but it can't stop the inertia and continues flying in a straight line away from the boat.

Leanne spins herself into a better position mid-air. She waits for the apex. She slows almost to a stop in the dangerous clouds, then swan dives back through the top of the air balloon toward The Blasted Dragon. She fires her grappling hook at the mast. The hook sets in and the automatic retrieval gear kicks in, pulling her to the ship. As she reels onto the ship, a glimmer in the sky catches her eyes. She recognizes the glint to be that of a Boeing Kaydet Model 75. She should know, she learned to fly in one of them. After all, they were the most common training plane on the planet at one point. Then she notices there are four of them. She lands with her feet against the mast. Then she drops down to the crow's nest, landing next to Robbie.

"We got big problems. There are four Kaydets headed this way," she says.

"What are Kaydets?" Robbie asks.

"Two-person bi-plane. Probably Hedgestone goons again. He really wants this ship."

"He wants the gold," Robbie says.

Leanne leaps over the crow's nest, shooting her grappling hook into the mast as she generates a free fall slow down. She lands on the deck with ease, then her TAC-COM retrieves the grappling hook back into its launching mechanism. Leanne runs up to the quarterdeck where Captain Cutthroat and Carrie are at the helm.

"We've got company. Four birds off the main bow," Leanne says.

Captain Cutthroat looks over to see the four objects flying at him.

"What are those?" he asks.

"They're called airplanes. Flying machines. More specifically, those are Boeing Kaydets. Bi-planes. It's a fix wing aircraft. One wing is fixed on the other wing. They are very fun to fly," Leanne says.

"You've flown one?" Captain Cutthroat asks.

"Yes. I trained in one when I was like 5 years old," Leanne says.

"Can cannons take them out?"

"Very easily," Leanne says.

Captain Cutthroat turns the helm, turning the ship broadside to the planes. He holds his arm out straight to his side, then aims his hand at the planes. Then, he counts to ten.

"They are moving pretty fast. No worries. I once took out five Royal Navy ships with two cannon balls. Okay, lass, listen up. You're at the helm now. Keep it straight. If the wind pushes in from the east, turn the ship left. Since the storm is on our left, we want to stay just on the outside of it. I think I'm going to lead them right into the storm," he says.

Captain Cutthroat rushes over to one of the cannons sitting on the main deck. Then he looks up at Robbie.

"How much power do those things have?" he asks.

"I'm only using about half their capacity," Robbie says.

"So if we want to be higher and faster, we can?" Captain Cutthroat asks.

"Yes. Much faster and much higher," Robbie says.

Captain Cutthroat smiles. Then he loads one cannon after another until all six cannons on the port side of the ship are loaded. He pulls a protractor from his inside coat pocket, setting it on the rail of the deck. Then he stands it up. There is a handle that looks like a lever to calculate the arch of the cannon. Captain Cutthroat measures the arch and then adjusts each cannon. He motions to Leanne to come and help him.

"I need you to tie these fuses together so I can fire all cannons at once. Then we're going to load this chain shot next. Maybe we can rip the wings off," Captain Cutthroat says.

Leanne looks down at two cannon balls that are chained to each other. Then she looks back up to see the oncoming planes. The pilots are well protected from the weather inside the planes. However, Team Adventure Club is at a disadvantage. The rain is pouring down on them in sheets. Leanne tries wiping the water off her face but it's no use, the rain is nonstop now.

CHAPTER 18

Jaxx, Scott, and Junior run as fast as they can over the sparse vegetation and small pools of water that are forming. Scott leaps over a low-lying palm tree that curves like an S, followed by Jaxx and Junior. Their boots kick up more sand and water as they push forward.

Jaxx watches as the flying pirate ship continues moving farther away from them. They run right up to the shoreline. They have to stop. The ocean sits before them. Jaxx pants loudly.

"That's it, boys. We're stuck here, I guess."

Mike slams into the ground, landing right behind them. The three men turn around to see their partner and are relieved.

"Guys, let's get to those jet skis on the outside of the island," Mike says.

"We should probably get back in the cave until this storm passes," Jaxx says.

"I don't know about you, but I want to get off this island," Junior says.

"Fine," Jaxx says.

"The jet skis are just around this bend. Let's go," Mike says.

Mike picks up Junior in a bear hug and lifts off. The jet pack moves quickly as Mike and Junior fly against the rain. Mike rounds the corner, holding Junior when he sees the jet skis still tied to the large rock. Without warning, he drops Junior as he still flies. Junior yells as he is let go, dropping into the sand and sliding to a stop on his head. His feet now dangle over him as he lies on his back.

"Thanks," Junior says, spitting sand out of his mouth.

He stands up, runs over to the jet skis, pulls out a utility knife, and slices the rope with ease. He unties the rope from the handle of Robbie's jet ski and then cuts both Leanne's and Carrie's free.

"Incoming!" Mike says.

Junior turns around just in time to get slammed by Scott, who crashes into him like a bowling ball. Junior and Scott flip over the jet ski onto the wet beach. Junior lies on his back in the shallow pool of water. Scott is having trouble standing up because he's laughing so hard.

"Man, the look on your face. 'Incoming!'" Scott says.

"Yes, very funny," Junior says. The men get to their feet, securing the jet skis. Scott looks them over and realizes they are not normal jet skis. They have digital screens and are shaped completely differently. They look like small bullet-shaped submarines. There are several ports on the console for USBs, a headphone jack, and a large square section that is missing a piece that looks like something plugs into it. Scott can't imagine what goes in that spot. Maybe a battery. Or a cell phone.

Junior pushes his out to the water, hopping on. The waves are kicking up badly and it's hard to hold on to the vehicle.

"If we don't move now, the waves are going to be too big for us to use these things," Junior says.

Mike comes around the corner, but this time he's holding Jaxx by his hands and Jaxx is skiing across the shallow water with his heels just touching the top of the water. Mike slows down and Jaxx goes from skiing to running as Mike lets him go. But Jaxx can't make his legs run as fast as he's moving and soon he trips, tumbling and rolling hard and fast into the sand. His head scoops up a bunch of sand, making a trench. Jaxx sits up, looking like he's wearing a night-time face mask made of pure sand.

"I bet that really exfoliates the pores," Scott says.

"Hey, don't judge. I also use a Clinique eye cream that gets rid of bags under your eyes," Jaxx says.

"No judgment, buddy," Scott says.

"Okay, less makeup advice and more riding on jet skis," Mike says.

"First of all, it's not makeup advice. It's self-care advice. You don't have a nighttime regimen?" Jaxx asks.

"Yeah, three melatonin and a quart of Benny and Jerry's 'Everything but the' ice cream," Mike says.

"That just sounds unhealthy," Scott says.

The men push the two remaining jet skis into the water, hopping on. Jaxx looks down at the console and realizes he doesn't know how to start the vehicle. He taps on the dark blank screen and it comes to life. The screen then goes to a series of dots and wants a pattern code put in. Jaxx pulls out a small square device from his belt pouch. The device looks like a portable drive that extends on both ends. Jaxx puts it over the screen and the device senses the fingerprint pattern and tries all possible combinations with those dots picks. It only takes a minute, and the device unlocks the jet ski.

The screen comes to life and a large red button appears that reads "START." Jaxx presses the button and the jet ski hums to life. He looks over at Junior, who has his jet ski up and running and is doing donuts in the water, waiting patiently.

Scott gets his jet ski going and the three of them line up. Mike leaps into the air and the jet pack ignites, letting Mike hover there for a moment. Then Mike signals for them to follow the ship and he takes off, flying over their heads. Jaxx, Scott, and Junior race after him. The jet skis are fast and they catch up to him with ease. The waves are getting much larger now and keeping the jet skis on top of the larger waves is becoming tough. Every other wave sends the men into the air about ten feet before they land on the rough water again. Mike, however, is having his own set of problems as the wind and rain are making it almost impossible for him to see where he is going. But his eyes are trained on the dot that is The Blasted Dragon in the air far ahead of them.

"We got this. We're going to win," Mike says.

Mike looks back at his men, who are criss-crossing the massive waves and flying into the air like a circus show. He knows driving a jet ski during a tropical storm is a bad idea, but they have to get to the ship at any cost. He pushes forward as the rain pelts his face.

Jaxx is looking at the console on the jet ski as it beeps and gives a weather advisory alert. The constant beeping is getting on his nerves.

"This thing won't shut up. I know there's a wave advisory warning, you dumb machine. I'm in it!" Jaxx says.

Jaxx studies the monitor for a moment when a new screen pops, that reads "Coastal Weather Advisory. Do you wish to go submersible? Then a green button appears on the screen." Jaxx pushes it and the jet ski handle pulls away from him and lowers. The seat extends backward, laying him on his stomach and a thick plastic dome rises up from the sides, sealing him in a dome. The monitor screen flips to a screen of vital signs. There is a dial for oxygen, depth, and speed. As well as a small radar on the top left of the screen. Then the jet ski dives underwater. Jaxx just holds on as he goes beneath the waves. Several lights blink to life and two large lights flip up, illuminating the ocean right before Jaxx's eyes. Jaxx is amazed at the technology. Then the sea is calm, and he is moving fast.

"Guys, go submersible with your jet skis," Jaxx says.

Jaxx looks to his left and sees Junior drop down into the deeper water, then Scott descends on his right. The three men are completely out of the storm and in awesome jet ski submarines.

"These are amazing. How much do these cost, I wonder," Scott says.

"Well, Hedgestone doesn't have these, that's for sure. What is Maxology Technology?" Junior asks.

"That's the manufacturer label on the console. They must be a state-of-the-art design company. Wait. These have to be Hedgestone's. Who else has the kind of money to create something as cool as this?" Scott asks. "I'm not even mad Mike took my jet pack. I'd rather have this."

Mike holds his hands up over his face as the rain has turned it a bright red. He is crying from the pain because it hurts so badly, but he is determined to reach the pirate ship. He looks back behind him for his teammates but doesn't see them. Then, out of a wave, Scott bursts through in his cool submarine jet ski. Mike sees the dome-covered awesomeness soar through the air and then back underwater again. Mike scans the water and can see Junior's and Jaxx's lights as they speed through the ocean.

"What are those?" Mike says.

Mike turns back around, pushing the button on the jet handle, accelerating toward the giant pirate ship just out of reach. Mike is flying fast now and close behind him Jaxx, Scott, and Junior launch out of the sea like dolphins playing in the waves.

"Let's go, guys!" Mike says.

CHAPTER 19

igh in the crow's nest, Robbie holds on for dear life as The Blasted Dragon is rocked by wind and rain. He is ever so vigilant, keeping an eye on the thrusters, watching for any signs of failure. The cold icy rain is slamming his head and body.

At the helm of the ship is the mighty Carrie Calusa. She holds onto the helm, steering the ship just on the outside of the storm like Captain Cutthroat instructed. She keeps what's left of the bowsprit pointed at the gray cloud line. But the updraft from the strong winds puts the ship almost on its side. Carrie knows the rudder, although very large, isn't made for flight. They need a wide rudder and maybe some wings on the side of the ship. But that's not going to happen. Carrie knows she has to concentrate.

Looking out to the port side, she can see the planes flying at them through the horrible dark clouds. When she sees several flashes of light. It doesn't take long for her to realize the planes are firing missiles at the balloon canopy.

"Hold tight. Incoming, port side," Carrie says.

Captain Cutthroat looks out to see the flying rockets coming at them. Then he feels the ship start to sway. He pushes against the rail in front of him. As does Leanne. Several crates and barrels start to roll and slide toward them. The ship creaks loudly, so loudly they can hear them over the rumbling thunder.

Those aren't heat-seeking missiles, so they must be firing by line of sight. I need to disrupt their trajectory or reduce my speed.

"Drop the mainsail," Carrie says.

Captain Cutthroat smiles, knowing she's going to reduce speed and, hopefully, the rockets will shoot in front of them. He does a somersault and then a round-off over a crate, getting to the mast in record time. He kicks the latch holding the mainsail up. The latch spins like a top and the mainsail drops like a rock. They slow down so quickly that every unsecured crate, barrel, weapon, tool, rope, and person flies forward. Leanne slides on the deck into a wooden riser that leads to the forecastle deck. She has just enough time to roll out of the way of a large barrel that slams into the riser, cracking open. Black powder pours out. Leanne wipes the water off her face as she watches four rockets soar past them just missing the balloon. She smiles.

"Hoist the mainsail," Carrie says.

Captain Cutthroat finds the rope attached to the yardarm that raises the mainsail and starts pulling it until the wind catches it, snatching it out of his hand. The sail extends, snapping into place. Captain Cutthroat catches the loose flying rope and ties it around the mast's lever arm.

Captain Cutthroat looks up as the four planes fly by between the balloon and the ship. They are all startled slightly as they rumble by. Carrie looks right at one of the pilots and it's Sir Oliver Hedgestone. He sneers at her. She smiles back at him as she waves.

"It's Hedgestone," Carrie says.

Leanne struggles to her feet. "Yeah, who else would it be?"

Leanne runs over to the cannons, meeting Captain Cutthroat next to them.

"I don't think I'll be able to get a shot off on these guys. Those things can maneuver better than expected," Captain Cutthroat says.

"I need to get in one," Leanne says.

"Well, seems like an impossible feat, m'lady," Captain Cutthroat says.

"Oh, I've done way crazier things," Leanne says.

"I do not doubt that," Captain Cutthroat says.

"Carrie, I have to get in one of those planes," Leanne says.

"Well, the only way that's going to happen is if you have a jet pack or something," Carrie says.

Just then, Mike crashes onto the deck of the ship, quickly getting up to his knees.

"I did it!" Mike says.

Captain Cutthroat pulls his sword as Mike stands up, pulling out the shock baton and activating the VeriShield. They are at a standoff, each with their weapons ready. Leanne finishes tying the fuses together, turning her attention to the two men.

Far above them, Robbie is still being beaten by the rain. He is busy carving something out of wood using his multi-tool when his TAC-COM starts to beep. It's a notification about the jet skis. He reads the screen that tells him that they are within remote operating distance. Robbie puts the two-inch carving in his pocket then taps on the screen of his TAC-COM and the camera screen activates, which activates the camera inside the jet ski. Robbie sees Scott's face.

"Hey, get off my jet ski," Robbie says.

Robbie sees Scott look around, then down at the screen. Scott's eyes go wide.

"Hey, you're that kid from the pirate ship," Scott says.

"I'm on the pirate ship and you're on my jet ski. Get off."

"Hey kid, it's like a hurricane out here. Maybe when I find some land you can have your jet ski back," Scott says.

"Why are you trying to kill us?" Robbie says.

"What? No. we're trying to save you from that crazy old man pirate guy."

"What? He's the good guy. You guys attacked us," Robbie says.

"What? No, we attacked him... ah... I see. But what are you talking about? Who are you kids?"

"We are Team Adventure Club. And you work for Sir Oliver Hedgestone, the most evil man on the planet," Robbie says.

"He wants the gold on the ship."

"Not his gold."

"Not yours, either," Scott says.

"Be that as it may. We are returning it to its rightful owners," Robbie says.

"If you're not careful, you're gonna return it to the bottom of the ocean," Scott says.

"Mister, this is real complicated stuff up here. And we're just kids trying to do the right thing. Maybe you should, too," Robbie says.

Scott stares at the monitor for a moment. "Darn it," Scott says.

The camera screen goes dark and Robbie darts around as he starts to worry more. *What did I just do? Are we really in trouble now? I mean, how much more trouble can we be in? We're only in a flying two-hundred-year-old pirate ship in a hurricane in the middle of a dogfight.*

Robbie stands up, leaning over the crow's nest. "I love my life!" He screams the words at the top of his lungs. Then ducks back down inside the crow's nest. He pulls out the carving. It is a dragon's head. Then he pulls the elastic tie line off his backpack. He threads the wooden dragon's head on the elastic rope, then he threads three large beads he also carved out of wood onto either side of the dragon's head. Then, he ties the rope at one end. He holds it up against the flame of the thrusters, melting the nylon elastic sealing tight. He pulls on it to see if it will expand without breaking, and it does. He puts it in his pocket.

Robbie stands up, looking out to see that the airplanes are circling back but now are approaching from the aft of the ship. He taps his TAC-COM, swiping screens until he gets to a red button and presses it. He looks up at the sky.

On the deck below, Captain Cutthroat and Mike are circling each other, waiting for the other to make the first move. Captain Cutthroat smiles the entire time. He is not worried about this man in the least. He's just trying not to kill him. He's not a killer. Never has been. Mike attacks. He slides in on one knee, holding the VeriShield above his head, and swinging the baton with his other arm.

Captain Cutthroat sees this move coming from a mile away. He's used the same move a million times. Captain Cutthroat kicks the VeriShield with such force it pushed Mike backward, but also knocks him off his feet. The captain drops to his back. But he's quick, rolling to his feet in a fluid movement. Sword fighting is similar to dance or ballet. One wrong move and you can twist an ankle.

Robbie yells from above them. "Incoming, from the aft!"

Carrie turns, looking behind her to see all four planes coming right at her. She's a sitting duck.

CHAPTER 20

The specialized research and development room is full of parts and tools that lie everywhere. The wall has robotic arms that assist with building new prototypes for use in foreign and domestic galactic warfare and to protect the inhabitants of the galaxies that Maximilian Bonnefield swore to protect from those who pose a threat. Max pulls the goggles off his eyes, placing them on his head as he stares at the electronic components in front of him. He stands up and walks over to a table that is littered with shiny metallic parts. He picks up what looks like a robot's arm and examines the joint as his TAC-COM sounds an alarm. Max looks at the device that he specially designed for himself and Team Adventure Club. The alarm flashes 911 and he knows it is an emergency.

Max runs out of the research and development room down the long, stark, white corridor to an elevator. Getting into the elevator, he presses the button for the seventh floor, which reads "HANGAR." The elevator moves just slightly, and the doors open to the seventh floor. Max runs out and down the wide hall, past space pilots in their uniforms. Several of the pilots wear normal pilot jumpsuits, but others have thicker suits with pads and helmets that have several hoses on them. Then there are the uniforms for the Bulvarians, a race of large, super-friendly aliens that look like they have armadillo skin and tails. Max runs past a Bulvarian who high-fives him. He runs to a door, swiping his card, and the door opens to a small room. Max runs in, opening a locker. Inside is a thick, orange-and-red flight suit. Below it on a shelf is a white helmet with a bubble visor. Max puts on the outfit as fast as he can. Then runs out of the room while putting on the helmet.

Max runs down another corridor to another room. He swipes his card, opening the door to a room where several operators sit behind computers. The operators all wear black uniforms, helmets, and dark black glasses. All three rows of eighteen operators turn to watch Max rush by, securing his hoses.

"Just me. Gotta run. I'll be doing a spacewalk to a free fall, FYI," Max says.

"A what?" one of the operators asks.

"Just open the door," Max says.

Max walks into a large, glass-enclosed room with a large, twenty-foot-high wall. The main door closes and seals. Max secures himself to a long metal bar that runs the length of the wall behind him.

Then, a moment later, the entire wall starts to open, revealing outer space. The station faces the sun and the blast of light is intense. Max turns, giving the operators a thumbs up.

"He can't be allowed to do this," one of the operators says.

"That's Maximilian Bonnefield. Without him, we wouldn't even have a planet," another operator says.

The operator nods, giving him a return thumbs up. Then she presses the depressurize button and the entire room that Max is in depressurizes. Then Max lifts into the air still attached to the secure bar. Max grabs the release lever, pushing it. He blasts out of the space station and into space, headed right for Earth. Max presses on his TAC-COM as he flies toward Earth. He swipes on his screen until he pulls up a screen with a universal space that can pinpoint any place in the universe. He then pings it to the position of Robbie's TAC-COM. On the screen, a green triangle blips in spinning, then a geological map of Earth pops up, triangulating Robbie's exact location, then locks on.

On the map screen, it looks as if the world adjusts to Max's location, but actually, Max's TAC-COM will guide him to Robbie's location. Then Max swipes his screen, pulling up a new screen that reads "JET PACK." Max pushes the power level up to yellow. The jet pack he is wearing activates with a massive thrust, shooting him even faster to Earth. Max puts his hands by his sides and his heads up display in his helmet locks onto Robbie.

"See you in four minutes, buddy," Max says.

Max flies toward Earth with the vastness of space behind him and the gigantic space station floating in the distance. Earth looks beautiful in the reflection of Max's visor. Then he sees the horrific, dark clouds of the tropical storm.

"Oh, good," Max says.

CHAPTER 21

Captain Cutthroat and Mike charge each other. Mike swings wildly and Captain Cutthroat sidesteps, kicking Mike in the side, pushing him off balance. Mike spins around, swinging again. Captain Cutthroat blocks the swing with his sword, which cuts the shock baton in half. Mike's eyes go wide as he stares at the disabled stick in his hand. Mike turns, leaping, but Captain Cutthroat grabs the top of the jet pack, pulling him back. Mike's feet land on the deck, and he tries to push off again. Captain Cutthroat reaches around Mike's shoulders, pulling the jet pack free, and rips the controller from his hand. Mike falls forward, sliding into the rails of the ship's deck.

Captain Cutthroat tosses the jet pack across the floor of the ship to Leanne. She rolls on her back and, as the jet pack slides toward her, she rolls over, sliding her arms into the straps, and stands up with the jet pack on.

Mike is cornered when he sees the MK-12 machine gun. He dives for it, but Leanne also sees it and dives, using the jet pack as a booster, getting to the gun before him. Leanne scoops up the gun in her hands like an eagle catching a field mouse. She spins upward to a hover. She racks the gun, aiming it at Mike.

"That's awesome! Sheer bliss," Captain Cutthroat says.

Mike stands with his hands up, then leaps over the rails of the ship. Leanne boosts over three feet to watch Mike fall, but just before he hits the ocean he tosses a Super Bouncy Bomb and it engulfs him, leaving his head, hands, and feet sticking out the rubberized ball. He floats on top of the waves, screaming, "Bad idea! Bad idea!"

Leanne looks up at Carrie, then past her. She sees the four planes coming. Without hesitation, Leanne blasts off, headed right for the planes. She flies past Carrie.

"I got this!"

Leanne is working overtime trying to keep the jet pack flying straight while fighting fifty-mile-an-hour winds and painful rain. But she's on a mission and nothing, not even a major rain-storm, will stop her. She is closing in on the air-planes, trying to get a plan together. Then she gets one. She dives down, dropping below the airplanes, but as she does, the planes fire four more rockets. Leanne almost has to duck to avoid them. Leanne spiral-spins, turning upward, get-ting a bead on the rockets. She fires the shock gun, hitting one of the rockets making it spin off course and crash into the massive waves below. The planes fly right over her head as she hovers in one spot.

On the ship, Carrie watches as the rockets fly at her. "Drop the mainsail," Carrie says.

Captain Cutthroat slides over to the lever, kicking it again. The sail drops and the ship slows down considerably. Then Carrie spins the rudder to the left and the ship banks hard. The first rocket misses the balloon. It feels like the ship has taken a year to turn.

"Brace for impact!" Carrie says. The helm is as far left as it can go. Carrie looks up and watches the second rocket miss the balloon. She notices that a rocket is missing, as the fourth rocket also misses the balloon. "They're trying to shoot us out of the sky," Carrie says.

"Hopefully that doesn't happen," Captain Cutthroat says.

Carrie stands spinning the wheel back the other way, trying to get them out of the storm. The ship is headed right into a very dark cloud and the rain and wind are picking up speed.

The planes fly overhead and just seconds behind is Leanne, right on their tail. She is firing the machine gun at one of the planes' rudders. Captain Cutthroat likes how the ship is lined up with the planes now. He rushes over to the starboard side of the ship, slamming his sword against the iron cleat on the rail of the ship, but the spark doesn't land. He tries again. No spark. Robbie looks down over the crow's nest, leaping out. His grappling hook slams into the mast of the ship, slowing his descent. He runs to Captain Cutthroat's side. He points his TAC-COM at the fuse, pressing the "laser" button. The thin red light ignites the fuse. They watch for a moment, then the cannon fires.

They look up, watching the cannonball fly through the air. It slams into the tail of one of the planes, knocking it out of commission. It spins out of control and into the ocean. Captain Cutthroat and Robbie cheer.

Then the floor of the ship leaves them as the ship drops about ten feet. They slam into the deck as they land. Robbie looks back at Carrie, who is not at the helm. Then, he sees her head pop up.

"What was that?" Robbie asks.

"No idea. The ship just dropped out of the air," Carrie says.

Carrie sees Leanne circling back to the ship. Carrie keeps the wheel tight as she holds to the starboard side, trying to keep the ship from listing more into the storm.

"It's like the ship is being sucked into the storm," Carrie says.

Captain Cutthroat runs up to the helm, taking over for Carrie.

"We're on the wrong side of the storm. The winds are spinning in. We have to pull out of this or the ship will be ripped apart," Captain Cutthroat says.

One of the planes flies overhead, as a large object falls toward the ship. Robbie looks up to see the bomb falling. He leaps off the ship in a dive as the bomb hits. The explosion blasts a hole in the deck of the ship, exposing the gold and jewels sitting in the hull. Robbie launches his grappling hook, and it slams into the back of the quarterdeck. Using his inertia, he swings back up to the port side of the quarterdeck. He lands next to Captain Cutthroat and Carrie.

"Hedgestone is trying to kill us," Robbie says.

"He's always trying to kill us!" Carrie says.

Leanne flies by super-fast and they barely hear her. "We're winning!" she says.

A plane flies up to the side of The Blasted Dragon, and the pilot looks over at them. It's Sir Oliver Hedgestone himself. He stares at Carrie for a moment, then his gaze is broken by the chest of a large man. Hedgestone refocuses to see Captain Cutthroat standing in front of her. Captain Cutthroat makes a slicing motion with his thumb across his neck. Hedgestone swallows a huge gulp and pulls back on the controls, lifting the plane up and away from the ship. Then he does a barrel roll away from the ship. Then, from right behind them, the other plane flies by them with a large hose attached to the side of the plane. The hose starts shooting black sticky goo at them. The wind and rain make it hard to shoot and most of the liquid goo sprays back onto the plane doing more damage to it than to The Blasted Dragon. The pilot pulls away.

Captain Cutthroat smacks Robbie on the shoulder, and they run over to the cannons.

"Let's take the rest out. What do you say?" Captain Cutthroat says.

Robbie fishes through his pocket, pulls out the necklace he made, and hands it to the captain.

"I made you this," Robbie says.

Captain Cutthroat looks in Robbie's hands at the well-crafted dragon head.

"That is fantastic! Thank you, Robbie," Captain Cutthroat says.

"Put it on," Robbie says.

Captain Cutthroat takes the necklace and slips it over his long stringy red hair and large head, hanging it around his neck. "I will treasure this always. Or until I die in the next ten minutes," Captain Cutthroat says.

"I hope we don't die in ten minutes. That'd be horrible," Robbie says.

Then they hear a loud thud behind them. Captain Cutthroat quickly turns around and sees a strange man in an orange and red flight suit and white helmet. Max leaps backward, away from the pirate.

"A pirate on a flying ship. No way!" Max says.

Robbie leaps up and runs to Max, giving him a huge hug. Captain Cutthroat steps back, disengaging, and watches the two hug.

"You made it. We are in a pickle," Robbie says.

"Clearly. Who's this, then?" Max asks.

"Uncle Max, meet Captain Cutthroat of The Blasted Dragon. Pirate of the seven seas starting in the year sixteen hundred and fifty-five until now," Robbie says.

"Wait, you're over two hundred years old?" Max asks.

"Yes. I am. Your nephew found me in a cave and now we are fighting strange men in flying machines who clearly want all my gold," Captain Cutthroat says.

Max looks down through the damaged hatch to the hull to see all the gold and jewels. Max can't believe his eyes. "Hedgestone in the plane?" Max asks.

"Yep," Robbie says.

Just then, sticky goo sprays the deck floor like machine-gun bullets. All three of them dive out of the way. Max ignites his jet pack flying into the air and after the plane.

"I'll get him!" Max says.

Carrie turns the wheel of the ship but it gets sucked in the dark part of the storm. Captain Cutthroat runs up the helm. "Better take cover, lass, this is going to get tricky," Captain Cutthroat says.

He stands up strong, gripping the steering wheel tightly in both hands. He shakes his hair out of his face like a supermodel.

"I've steered The Blasted Dragon through many a storm. There ain't no storm she can't handle. Although never in the air attached to a balloon. So let's see what happens. Grrrr."

The ship dips into another air pocket, dropping a little. The rain pours on the ship like it's a play toy in the shower. The wind slams against them, spinning the aft of the ship around and catching them in a swirling vortex of turbulent clouds. Carrie slides into a large crate, knocking it loose. She and the crate slide to the port side of the ship. She holds on for dear life. Robbie, having made it back to the mast of the ship, holds onto a long rope wrapped around the long piece of wood sticking out of the ship.

Captain Cutthroat turns the wheel to the starboard side, but the ship continues to spin in the opposite direction. The wind slams the sails and the balloon. The Blast Dragon lifts and drops just like it's on the ocean. But now it's in a slow spin. The rain is relentless and has been for thirty minutes. Captain Cutthroat looks out into the dark clouds, watching the lightning flash in the sky. He smiles wide and laughs out loud. "I love being a pirate," he says.

CHAPTER 22

Max looks behind himself and sees the ship disappear into the dark, menacing clouds. He turns his attention back to catching Hedgestone, who flies straight up into the air with no worries. Max is right behind him like Iron Man. Max catches up to him and is right outside his window. Grabbing the support bar holding the fixed wings, Max knocks on the pilot's side window.

Hedgestone looks over to see Max on the outside.

"Pull over. Just kidding. I'm going to hurt you real good, Hedgestone. Don't you ever learn? Don't mess with Team Adventure Club!" Max says.

"*You* don't learn, Maximilian. I'm a billionaire and I can do whatever I want. That treasure is mine and you and those bratty kids can't stop me," Hedgestone says.

Max punches the window, shattering it. He grabs Hedgestone by the shirt. But Hedgestone cuts the engine to the plane, and it changes direction quite quickly. Max lets him go and watches the plane fall beneath him.

Max turns, diving at the plane as it free-falls awkwardly in the sky. Max zooms in on the plane, but Hedgestone kicks the engine on and barrel rolls out of the path of Max. The plane goes into an upside-down arc, circling back into a level position, heading right for Max. Max smiles, letting Hedgestone chase him right into the storm.

Max looks over at Leanne spiraling around the other plane like a Maypole streamer. Leanne comes back up over the plane again, landing on the top of it. She makes her way to the pilot, who is protected by a piece of glass shaped like a bubble. She fires her grappling hook into the canopy, then wrenches it off the plane completely.

"Get out," Leanne says. The pilot screams, jumping out of the plane. Leanne hops in the pilot's seat and is a little cramped. Wearing the jet pack makes it hard for her to fit in the seat. She stands up, takes off the jet pack, and puts it in the gunner's seat behind her. She hops in the pilot seat, taking control of the Boeing Stearman Model 75 Kaydet. She accelerates, making a beeline for Hedgestone's plane. Max turns toward her. He's leading Hedgestone right into a trap. He flies faster, so Hedgestone flies faster. Leanne sees Max coming at her with Hedgestone on his tail. She steadies the controls by tying a hair tie to the steering handle and the latch to the broken window. Kneeling on the seat, she waits for the right moment. She is constantly wiping rain from her face. Squinting, she can see Max is almost to her. As he flies over her, Leanne stands, grabs the jet pack, and leaps out of the plane.

Hedgestone doesn't figure out Leanne's plan until it's too late. The front of Leanne's plane collides with the tail of Hedgestone's plane, cutting it in half. Hedgestone wastes no time leaping out of his plane into the cold, rough ocean below. Leanne and Max watch as Hedgestone's parachute opens, and he floats into the chaotic waters below.

Max and Leanne match speed, high-fiving each other.

"Where's the ship?" Leanne asks.

"In the storm. We have to go into the storm, Leanne. It might get way crazy," Max says.

"Hopefully," she says.

CHAPTER 23

Captain Cutthroat steers the ship as best he can, but he is up against something he's never had to deal with before. Flying. The ship swings from side to side as it lifts up and drops. The rain seems to be hitting them from every direction. He spins the wheel one way, and then the other.

"Hoist the mainsail. Hoist all port side lower mast sails," Captain Cutthroat says.

Robbie has no idea what he is talking about. "What?" Robbie asks.

"See those small yard arms sticking out there? They're on all the masts. Pop those sails."

Robbie runs to the foremast, kicking the lever, and the sail pops up. He runs to the mainmast, releasing that yardarm, and the sail pops up. Then he runs to the mizzenmast on the aft of the ship, releasing that sail as well. The ship cuts so hard to the port side that it rises about forty degrees sideways. Every loose crate, barrel, and item rolls off the ship to the rocky waters below.

As Captain Cutthroat steadies the ship, Max and Leanne fly right up the deck, landing hard. The wet deck causes both of them to slide onto the quarterdeck. Max catches Leanne, cradling her in his arms. "I got ya," Max says.

Max runs up to the helm and stands next to Captain Cutthroat. Leanne joins them.

"I can't steer this thing. I need a larger rudder," Captain Cutthroat says.

Max thinks for a moment. "Leanne, follow my lead. Let's go!" Max says.

Max runs, followed by Leanne, and leaps over the ship. They fly to the aft of the ship. Max leans against the ship with his hands. Leanne does the same thing.

"Okay, use your jet pack to push this ship out of the storm," Max says.

Leanne nods and together they accelerate their packs to full power. The Blasted Dragon lunges forward with gusto. Carrie rolls toward the quarterdeck, catching herself with a loose rope hanging off the wooden rails.

Captain Cutthroat smiles as the ship speeds up. The wind and rain smacking him in the face makes him feel whole again. He had forgotten how much he enjoys the open sea. Or well, now, the open air. He holds on tightly to the helm, closing his eyes. He thinks of the days long past and his old crewmen, he was proud to call ship-mates. Men, he called friends. They are all gone, for hundreds of years now. He can smell the old world if only for a brief second. He recalls the flavor of the spice islands and how much he misses garlic and olives. If nothing else, he knows this is his last voyage. The last time he will be the captain of The Blasted Dragon, a ship that he's called home for far too long. Then he hears a snap. A rope. But which one? He sees it whipping around freely snapping in the air.

The rope on the port side of the balloon has snapped, letting the balloon wobble dangerously. Captain Cutthroat shifts his attention to the other rope connecting the bow to the balloon. It is extremely tight now. And all the rain has made the rope contract tighter than it normally does.

Everyone feels the boat rock. Max and Leanne slam their heads into the back of the captain's quarters. Carrie is still holding onto the rope. Robbie is now making his way to the bow of the ship to try to secure the flailing rope. Robbie looks over as the other rope snaps. The bow of the ship falls down about ten degrees. The balloon shoots up, pulling the aft of the ship upward. One of the ropes on the center mast snaps as well, on the starboard side. The boat rolls to its port side.

Carrie is holding on for dear life as she is knocked around by the failing support ropes. Max and Leanne fly up over the aft quarterdeck, landing behind Captain Cutthroat. Max sees the hanging ship and quickly looks around for other weaknesses.

"These ropes are going to snap. Seems our future is imminent, my friend," Captain Cutthroat says.

Robbie swings back to the mainmast using his grappling hook. He rushes up the ladder to the crow's nest. He reaches the nest, dropping the force of the thrusters. The ship starts to descend. The wind can't get any stronger than it is right now. Robbie looks out ahead of them and only sees dark clouds. He continues to reduce the thrust of the engines and the ship continues to lower.

Captain Cutthroat knows what Robbie is up to. They don't stand much of a chance in the rough waves of the storm, but at least they stand some chance. Up here, if the ship drops, they don't have a chance at all.

"Robbie, drop her. I'll get through the waves," Captain Cutthroat says.

Robbie turns back to the thrusters and decreases the power even more. They are quickly lowering. And Robbie can see the high waves of the raging waters getting close.

The aft mast rope snaps behind them, whipping the rope right at their heads. They all duck and the rope snaps into the far rail on the port side, cracking it in half. The boat rocks back a little as the weight distribution is now uneven.

"Not long now," Max says.

Captain Cutthroat knows what he has to do. He walks over to the side of the ship, looking down. It's a far drop for sure. He has to wait a little longer. He looks up at Robbie, who is watching his every move. He motions to him to slow down again. Robbie reduces speed, and the ship is now only fifteen feet above the highest wave. Captain Cutthroat walks back over to the helm, grabbing it tightly.

"Max, Leanne. When I say so, cut those two remaining ropes," he says.

Max is ready. Leanne leaps with a jet pack burst, landing next to the rope in the middle on the port side. Captain Cutthroat looks up at Robbie, nodding his head.

"Now, dear boy."

Robbie cuts the thrusters just as Max and Leanne cut the ropes. The boat drops like a rock. It falls fast, slamming the water on a high wave with a massive splash. The bow of the ship dips down on the wave at a sixty-degree angle. They are staring straight down at the sea. Then the ship's bow rises up so they are now forty degrees the other way. Max and Leanne stay in the air with their jet packs on, while Carrie feels like she's riding a bull in a rodeo. Robbie just braces himself inside the crow's nest, hoping for the best.

The noise of the gold and jewels crashing around in the hull is deafening, even against the storm and crashing waves. The Blasted Dragon rises and falls with great heights, sometimes over a hundred feet. Right now, Captain Cutthroat is proving why he is known as one of the best captains to have ever lived. He steers them away from an oncoming wave time and time again. Until finally they see sunlight. The storm is breaking, and the waves are calming down.

The ship sails right into the harbor of the Ka Wai Anuanu, crashing into several floating hotel rooms. Then it slams against the shoreline digging a long deep trench. The boat is so heavy that not even the paved road can stop it. The ship continues to slide across the island and into the lobby of the expensive resort.

Tourists run for cover as the massive ship crashes through the four-story window of the beautiful lobby, coming to a stop. Captain

Cutthroat is tossed to the deck. Robbie stays huddled as he gets covered in broken glass.

Max and Leanne fly in, landing inside the lobby of the resort. A manager comes running up.

"Oh, my. What is going on? Is that a pirate ship? Who are you guys? Where did you come from? Did you come from the storm?" the manager questions.

"Okay. Let's just go over here and we can talk about it," Max says.

Max walks the manager away from the debris.

Robbie looks out over the crow's nest and sees that they are now inside the lobby. He crawls down to the deck to Captain Cutthroat, who is getting to his feet.

"That was the most fun I've had in so many years," Captain Cutthroat says.

"Well, that was just a holiday weekend for us," Robbie says.

Leanne lands next to them on the boat as Carrie walks up to them.

"Well, I guess this is where my journey ends, kids," Captain Cutthroat says.

Just then, Sir Oliver Hedgestone flies in with his own jet pack hovering over them.

"Step away from the treasure, you crazy kids!" Hedgestone says.

Hedgestone opens fire with a shock pistol, shooting electrically charged projectiles at them. He hits Captain Cutthroat two times. Captain Cutthroat goes to jump off the ship, but he still can't leave the ship.

Leanne takes off her jet pack, handing it to the captain.

"No one said you can't fly off the ship," Leanne says.

Captain Cutthroat slings the jet pack on lifting off the ship. He seems to be okay. Hedgestone watches as the large man of a pirate rises into the air.

"It's working," Robbie says.

Captain Cutthroat starts after Hedgestone, catching him outside. Carrie, Robbie, and Leanne watch as the pirate chases Sir Oliver Hedgestone around the resort in their jet packs.

The three of them leap off the ship, firing their grappling hooks into the side of the ship lowering themselves to the lobby floor fifty feet below.

A tourist couple stands in the lobby in shock. The man, who is wearing a Hawaiian shirt, starts clapping. "I will be coming back here next year. This place is awesome!"

Robbie looks around at the damage and the ship.

"We have to get that treasure out of there before someone tries and takes it," Robbie says.

"Leave that up to us," Scott says.

Robbie turns around to see Scott, Jaxx, and Junior standing there.

"We left your jet skis over at the dock that the ship didn't damage," he says.

"What? Awesome," Robbie says.

"Look, we heard what you said. And we aren't in the habit of fighting children, regardless of how awesome they are. You guys did some pretty amazing things today. And after talking about it, we decided that if you ever need any help, you know, protecting the Earth, look us up. We'd be happy to help," Scott says.

"Where's your other buddy?" Carrie asks.

"Mike, he's a great guy. Don't worry about him. I mean, he's floating in the ocean at the moment in a super-sized rubber ball. We'll just let him float out there a while, then we'll go get him," Scott says.

Scott and his team shake Carrie's, Leanne's, and Robbie's hands, then turn and walk away.

Max walks up to the gang, grabbing them all in a hug.

"Okay, well, the manager isn't happy, but I promised him it'd all be paid for. Not by us, but by the National Treasure Recovery Team, or whatever. I don't know. I made it up. I'm sure, like, two of those gold pots are more than enough to cover the cost of this mess," Max says.

Captain Cutthroat lands next to the gang and Max. He stands there for a moment looking down at his feet. He can't believe he's off the ship. He takes the jet pack off, handing it back to Leanne. Then a blue burst of light expands from the necklace and over Captain Cutthroat's body. Captain Cutthroat pulls on the necklace and smiles.

"Robbie, the necklace works. How did you know?"

"I didn't, but I figured if you can't leave the ship, then maybe the ship can come with you. So I took part of the mainmast and carved a dragon's head and some beads," Robbie says.

"Well, this has been the most exhilarating day of my life in a long time. But now I'm a pirate without a ship and I guess the authorities will confiscate the gold and gems. So I'm penniless. But I'm happy to get a fresh start. Maybe explore the new world."

"Well, if you really want to explore, I can offer you a spot on my team. Even if just for a little bit," Max says.

"What do you do? Besides show up out of nowhere and save the day?" Captain Cutthroat asks.

"I work in space."

"Space? Like up there. Where the stars are?"

"Yeah, there are plenty of ships that need a captain up there. And just think of all the other planets you can explore," Max says.

"I'll have to think about... yes. Yes, take me to space. I will then be a space pirate."

"See, he gets it," Max says.

"You kids are something else," Captain Cutthroat says.

Captain Cutthroat walks away. "Don't go anywhere," he says.

They stand there waiting while Max talks on a cell phone. Captain Cutthroat returns with four small chests made of wood. He puts them down on a table in the lobby.

"Pick one," he says.

Carrie reaches out, picking one up. As do Leanne and Robbie. They leave one on the table for Uncle Max.

"Open them," Captain Cutthroat says.

They open their chests and their faces shine with a golden hue. They all smile widely. Then

Captain Cutthroat pulls out the winged helmet Robbie was so fascinated with.

" We can keep all this?" Robbie asks.

"Yeah, who cares. It's long-lost treasure," Captain Cutthroat says.

Max walks up, putting his cellphone away. "You're all good, sir. You can leave with me whenever you're ready," Max says.

"What about my ship and the treasure?" Captain Cutthroat asks.

"I took care of it. Your stuff will be inventoried and cataloged. The ship will be removed and placed in storage. As far as anyone will know, this is all from a movie set. Looks real, but it's all fake," Max says.

Captain Cutthroat hugs Team Adventure Club one last time. Two black SUVs show up. Two men in black suits get out. Max nods to the men, motioning to Captain Cutthroat. They walk over to the vehicles, getting in. Carrie, Leanne, and Robbie watch the SUVs pull away.

They start walking back to the docks where their jet skis are. Robbie looks back to see the massive ship sticking half out of the building and smiles.

"What do you guys want to do next weekend?" Robbie says.

"I've been reading up on this story about a group of scientists stuck on an island full of robots."

"That sounds fun," Carrie says.

"I hate robots. So yeah, let's go do that," Robbie says.

They laugh, hopping on their jet skis, starting them. They rev up their engines, turn the jet skis around, and head home.

Another adventure in the books. But that's nothing new for one of the coolest clubs in the world: Team Adventure Club. Job well done.

END

BOOK CLUB QUESTIONS

1. What was your favorite part of Captain Cutthroat's Revenge?

2. Did the story keep you involved?

3. What enemy would you like to see Team Adventure Club fight?

4. If you could design a new tool for Robbie, what would it be?

5. Does Carrie make a good leader?

6. Would you like to see Captain Cutthroat join Team Adventure Club permanently?

7. Do all the characters of Team Adventure Club get enough page time?

8. If you were in Team Adventure Club who one skill would you bring?

9. Who is crazier, Uncle Max or Leanne?

10. What's the craziest thing you've ever done?

Author Bio

Joe Davison is widely known for his co-starring role on Stranger Things. However, his work spans over two decades. He has written over thirty-five screenplays and directed 8 feature films such as the *Horror Comedy, Sorority of the Damned* starring Felissa Rose, the *Horror Thriller, Frost Bite*, and *As Night Falls* starring Debbie Rochon. His credits as a writer include the recently released young adult adventure series *Team Adventure Club*, as well as *Cold Front* and the just-released supernatural crime noir series *Mike Strong: For Hire*.

Discover more at
4HorsemenPublications.com

10% off using HORSEMEN10

www.ingramcontent.com/pod-product-compliance
Lightning Source LLC
Chambersburg PA
CBHW061537310726
48972CB00008B/2493